# Between the Realms

## By Lorraine Carey

# The Inspiration

The 1970s was a golden era that resonates deeply with us baby boomers and remains a cherished chapter in our lives. It was a time of unparalleled rock music, vibrant clubs pulsing with energy, and the exhilaration of open-air concerts beneath starlit skies. For me, those years witnessed the emergence of an intense passion as I embraced the role of a groupie—albeit one on the milder side—and unapologetically immersed myself in the world of music.

In those moments, standing at the stage, I felt an emotional connection, a fusion of rhythm in my soul that moved not just my body but my entire being. With my dear girlfriends at my side, we danced with an uncontainable fervor, swept away by tunes and lyrics that would define a generation. I was a dedicated disciple of the music scene and didn't miss a single concert in my vicinity.

I must confess here: the enigmatic guitarists had a penchant for strumming their way into my heart. Their fingers played the soul-stirring notes, holding an irresistible allure and powerful magnetism that was an unexpected turn-on. My journey led to fleeting encounters with several band members from the local area and beyond, yet these romances fizzled as quickly as they'd ignited. What remained unwavering was my profound adoration for the era that provided a treasure trove of memories enough to last a lifetime.

It is from this fountain of passion that my tale took root. The desire to recapture that era's essence, vivacity, and fervor propelled me to craft Jennifer Kovich and Dylan Anderson's story.

These two characters encapsulate the very spirit of the seventies, and their souls are interwoven with the same love for that remarkable time. As I pen their journey, I embark upon a mission to channel the magic of the past and share a narrative that radiates the timeless splendor of an era that will forever occupy a special place in my heart.

I wish I could go back, even for just a short time, to bask in the glorious seventies.

# Chapter 1

*Dylan Anderson 2023*

My heartbeat quickens as I descend the stairs to my music studio. I know I probably should update this old place, but it makes me feel peaceful every time I come here. It's like I can almost see the guys in here with me rehearsing for an upcoming gig.

I sit in my ripped leather office chair and roll back to the shelf where I store my old eight-track tapes, ready to relive some memories, but the dust and dampness in the air permeate my nostrils, bringing on a sneezing fit. I guess that's all part of having a studio in your basement.

I shake my head and glance over at the old Fender Vintera and Polymoog synthesizer patiently waiting. It's been some forty-six years since I was the lead guitarist for Ablaze. Even though we were a local band from the Youngstown area, most living in Ohio had heard of us. We had planned on going big time, but it never happened, we remained a respected and popular local band.

I open the top drawer of my desk and pull out a box containing CDs of the band's most popular songs. I'm glad I had those old eight-tracks converted. I make a mental note to send one to Jennifer Kovich. She's one of the main reasons I've been learning how to time travel. We were young and in love back in the 70s. I've spent the last two years reminiscing about the times we shared before she broke my heart. But things were about to change.  I hope she has a CD player. If not, I'll have to go to plan B, which is more of an upfront and personal approach that could be dangerous for both of us. Either way, I'm feeling positive about the spell that will propel her back to 1976. And I'll be back there as well, waiting.

It's been a long time since I've felt so alive.

I think about what Troy Duncan, Grand Master had taught me these past few years at the Orion's Path meetings I was attending. I met Troy at a party one night back in the early seventies, and he said he was starting some New Age club. I even told Jennifer about it, but I believe she never had much interest. I guess she wasn't into astrology at the time, but that was only a cover for whatwent on in that group.

When I first heard about it, I thought I was attending some sort of astrology club, but I was wrong. I learned so much there. If not for Gregg, our former drummer, I'd have no idea that time travel could be achieved simply by playing certain notes on a musical instrument to generate a high vibrational frequency. All along, I thought something like that could only be attained by playing a heavy metal song backward on the old vinyl while listening for the embedded codes. I presume he did some deep diving after retiring from teaching science at the local high school, here in Canfield, Ohio. It was here, in this modest log-style cabin out in the Ohio countryside, that I became a devout member and learned what I'd do with my newfound knowledge of time travel.

I've been planning this for two years now. My dreams are about to come true as long as I follow the instructions to the letter. Hell, no one will even miss me. It's been five years since my divorce, and I have no children, which leaves me with no reason to reconsider my decision. Mom and Dad both passed away years ago, and I've never had much contact with my sister, who now lives in Pittsburg. Plus, it's a different world now, one I feel as if I don't belong in. Who could've predicted forty years ago that everything could change so much?

If all goes according to plan, I'll be transported back to 1976 with the band and my buddies playing at local clubs, including the famous Regal Room Club in Struthers, Ohio. I'll be twenty-three again and able to relive the best years of my life, including the time when I met Jennifer. I've been thinking of her even more so since the divorce. She and I weren't just a passing thing. I hoped we'd end up together, but fate chose a different path for the both of us. Now, I have the tools to change our destiny, and I'm more than ready to make the journey back.

The instructions I learned to open the time portal will have consequences for Jennifer and me. Once I return to the seventies, I'll have no means of getting back, although I highly doubt, I'd want to return. I mean, I've spent two years learning and plotting how to create this time travel spell, and my mind is set. Besides, I've always felt as if I don't belong in this modern world.

According to Troy, the Grand Master, I will be transported back to the exact time, to the very night I met Jennifer in a club where the band was due to perform.

As for Jennifer, who knows if she'll be able to journey back. Will she even want to? I hope that once we are reunited, she'll see it was all meant to be.

That's the deal, the one I made with Troy…or should I say the one I made with the devil? Is it fair that she might not have the means to return to her current life? I don't care. I guess it's selfish of me, but I long to get those years back, and I'm more than happy to pay the price.

It's not that I've been stalking Jennifer for years on social media—I'm just keeping abreast of what's been going on in her life.

Okay, I guess I have to admit I'm obsessed with her. I learned she'd separated from her husband and was now writing romance books for a living. She retired from teaching a few years back, and I have now retired from operating a local landscaping company. She is sixty-nine but still a looker, based on the pictures she posts on social media.

She moved to St. Petersburg, Florida, while I remained here in Canfield, Ohio. As I check her daughter Brandy's photos, I see the resemblance. She has the same strawberry blonde hair and intoxicating green eyes as her mother.

My mind wanders back to the first night we met. I was on stage, playing with Ablaze, our band, at the Regal Room. It was fall, and everyone's mood was lighter after having suffered through a humid summer. Being their lead guitarist, I was playing right up front, and I noticed an attractive, petite blonde dancing with another girl as we played Grand Funk Railroad's hit, "Heartbreaker." I watched her as she swayed back and forth in her hip-hugger jeans and revealing yellow halter top. She looked at me, and I winked at her. She smiled at me and moved closer to the edge of the stage. Our break was coming up next, and I thought, *I'll make damn sure I get to know that chick.*

It was as though a hot poker shot through me when I looked into her eyes and asked if I could buy her a drink. There was chemistry there, for sure. We sat at the bar and chatted. I got lost in her emerald eyes as she spoke of her college classes and her hopes of becoming a teacher. She had just finished her last year of college and wanted to do some substitute teaching in the area. She was a local girl but seemed so different from the other girls I'd dated in the area. She had goals, while most of the others just wanted to snag a husband and have babies.

Our drummer and my best friend, Gregg motioned that it was time for the second show. I told Jennifer to leave me her number as I planned on asking her out—mind you, this was back in the Stone Age when we didn't have cell phones. She wrote her number on a small cocktail napkin from the bar, and I tucked it away in my jeans pocket. That was the beginning of our short-lived love affair.

The more I thought about her, the more I knew I had to practice the routine to open the portal. To do so, I had to play the E4 chord on my old Fender Vintera thirteen times as I recited the chant Troy had taught me. I had to sing it in a high-pitched, E-5 falsetto, the highest note achievable for men, according to him. I decided to put it at the end of the recording I planned to put on the CD and I'd mail it to Jennifer.

I was told I needed to have three items with me belonging to that period and needed to be somewhere near Jennifer and I frequented back in the day. That was a no-brainer: the Regal Room, a once thriving dance club, but now simply an abandoned building. It was sad to see this club falling into such disrepair.

I scoped out the area a few nights ago, climbed over the rusty chain link fence, and found no sign of security cameras, so I knew it would be easy to pull this off.

I pull out an old vinyl record—one of the few local hits from way back—set it on the vintage player and sink back into my chair as I listen to "Dark Wicked Woman," one of our originals, and envision Jennifer in the club on the dance floor, illuminated by beams of colored lights.

*It won't be long now, my love, not long. Just a few more solo rehearsals and everything will be set into motion. We'll be back where we belong, in the era meant for us. I think you'll soon realize this as well.*

# Chapter 2



I finish my power walk around the neighborhood as the sun is about to set. September is my favorite time of the year, when the Florida evenings are still warm, and a walk always lifts my spirits. I sit down and unplug my earbuds the minute I get in the door, and check my messages, hoping to hear from my best friend, Laney Morrison. We'd been so close after teaching together.

We are supposed to have lunch this Saturday. Lord knows I need to get out of the house and have some real human interaction. It's been eight years since I retired as a fourth-grade teacher and started my career as an indie romance author—talk about a lonely hobby. Most of my friends these days are other authors I've met online.

My daughter, Brandy, and I are close. She usually calls every other day to check on me. The last time we saw each other was before she moved to South Carolina in July. I know she worries about me, especially since her dad, Mark, and I got a legal separation a year ago. These days, she's busy with her work as a physical therapist, and she spends the evenings with her live-in boyfriend, Brian.

My stomach rumbles, demanding food, but I want a hot shower first. The water is warm as it sprays down on my skin. I close my eyes, and for some reason, I think about Mark, wondering what he's up to these days. Hell, he's just a half-hour's drive away in Tampa, but it feels as though he's moved to the other end of the world. It's been months since I've even had a call from him, but I do know he phones Brandy every week. When I ask her how he's doing, she's always vague. Either she doesn't want to tell me the truth or admit to the fact that he doesn't share anything with her. That's part of the reason behind our separation—the lack of communication. He was still working and had quite a few out-of-town business trips, and I was stuck at home, working on my third book. When he returned from his trips, I'd question him on how the trip was, but he always took it the wrong way and said I was interrogating him.

In the back of my mind, I always knew he was cheating on me. Call it intuition if you will.

I wrap my towel around myself and head to the kitchen to heat a Lean Cuisine meal. I don't feel like cooking tonight. I lost my desire to cook when Mark left. Why bother cooking for one person?

I slip into my silk pajamas and eat my dinner. I pour a glass of wine while scanning Facebook. As I check out the Youngstown hometown page, I notice that someone has posted a video of Ablaze from back in 1976, when they first played at Midway Park. I was at that concert!

I play the video, watching intently as the band plays one of their hits, my eyes fixed on Dylan Anderson, the lead guitarist. A hot rush runs through me as I watch him, playing and singing, his long, brown, shag-style hair whipping from side to side. *Where has the time gone? Seems like yesterday when I was quite the social butterfly enjoying outings with my friends and going to these concerts. Some even called me the 'It Girl'.* I sigh thinking how much time I spend alone now, sitting in this house. I have my writing but there's still a void here. I miss my students and the interaction with them when I worked. I was called last year to see if I wanted to substitute or volunteer, but I declined. Knowing about this new era of teaching and younger teachers has me feeling a bit intimidated, I feel I wouldn't fit in. I figure my time has passed and I've lost my Mojo lately.

My mind wanders back to when I met Dylan shortly after one of his performances. I've always been turned on by musicians for some reason, so it's no surprise that Dylan and I started dating soon after we met. Those were good times.

I sigh and close my eyes, remembering how I'd follow the band to each venue and how Dylan and I would get together after the shows. I danced to the music with Tracey Blaznick, my good friend since high school. I was convinced that every song Dylan sang, he sang it for me.

The louder the music, the more my body responded. It was as if I had center stage, and it wasn't uncommon to have a few guys watching me.

I loved dancing. Dylan said I was good at it and should pursue it as a career, but I had just graduated from Youngstown State University with a teaching degree and was excited to start teaching. I'd like to think dancing was a hobby.

After the show, we usually had a few drinks and ended up back at the apartment he shared with Gregg, the band's drummer. A few tokes on some decent pot later, and we'd have sex—good sex. I felt as if I was special, getting to be with a hot, local musician, but my mother wasn't too fond of him, always warning me about the flashy lifestyle musicians led.

I'm compelled to play the video again, paying more attention to the crowd this time, hoping I'll see myself there. I usually wore hip-hugger jeans, while my strawberry blonde hair falling way below my shoulders made it pretty easy to pick me out in a crowd. Those were the good times—we had no social media or cell phones to distract us, and we lived in real-time in the real world. How I wish things were still that simple.

After a second glass of wine, I start to feel drowsy, so I close the laptop and head for bed…alone.

I'll message Laney tomorrow.

# Chapter 3

*Jennifer 2023*

I woke up feeling the effects of the two glasses of wine I had last night. My mouth feels as if I've ingested a few cotton balls, and my head is throbbing. I need coffee.

I slip out of my pajamas and stand in front of my full-length mirror, looking at my naked body and experiencing flashbacks of Dylan, along with a strong urge to pleasure myself.

After throwing on my comfy robe, I head to the kitchen for some of my favorite mocha brew and sit at the modern-style glass kitchen table, staring at my laptop, knowing I have to work on my book. It's been two weeks since I'd written a few sentences. This particular romance thriller has left me stumped. *Maybe a call to Laney will get me motivated. What I really need is a ladies' day out.*

I glance at the large clock on the wall with its bold Roman numerals. It's already 9 a.m. I know Laney will be up. She's an early riser, just like me.

It's good to hear her voice, but she's quick to pick up the anxious tone in mine. "What's with you? You sound excited."

"I gotta tell ya, it's weird…I mean, odd." I hesitate for a moment wondering if I should divulge my secret.

"What? What's weird?"

"Okay—you're not going to believe this, but as I was watching a video on Facebook, I relived the seventies again with an old boyfriend."

"What's so weird about that?"

"Well, for one, I haven't thought of this guy in years, and I mean, I could envision almost every detail I spent with him back then, even down to what I was wearing." There's a moment of silence on the other end of the phone. "You still there?"

"Of course, I am. I'm just listening. Want to know what I think?"

"What?"

"I think you need to get out more. I mean, I know we have our yoga class, and you have your writing, but you need more human contact," Laney says.

"I have to agree with you. I know I spend too many hours in this house sitting at this table, writing, or staring out the window hoping to get a surge of inspiration.  At least you get out a few days a week helping out at the women's shelter."

"Yes, and it does me a world of good. Have you ever considered a ladies' weekend getaway?"

"Not really. I had more like a ladies' day or night in mind—what, exactly, are you thinking?" I ask.

Laney's response comes quickly: "Nothing outrageous. Maybe a short trip to Virginia Beach or something."

"It'll be October soon. I think the water might be a bit cold," I counter.

"It's not the water we're going for, girl. It's to get you out of your rut. We could enjoy the shops and restaurants and even venture out to some of the clubs."

"Oh, that sounds like me," I joke. *If she only knew that younger version of me from a world gone by.*

I hear Laney's deep sigh over the phone. "No, seriously—just think about it. You know, you and I have spent the past thirty years teaching together. We know each other pretty well, but damn, you never told me about this guy."

I take a deep breath. "It was so long ago. He was the lead guitarist in a local band, and I had a thing for musicians."

"A groupie, huh?"

"Maybe just a little, but I loved to dance to the live music of the band. We dated for several months before I met Mark."

"Was he hot?"

"He was back then."

"You mean you haven't seen any recent pics?"

"Well, I did take a look at his Facebook page a few times, but that was it. He looks good for sixty-eight. The long brown shag is gone, but he looks to be in good shape."

"Single? Divorced?" Laney asks, her interest peaking.

"I believe his page said divorced."

"Ah-ha! So, you have done some snooping…or should I say stalking?"

I stifle a laugh. I can't tell her the naughty thoughts I've had recently, or she'd think I opened the wine bottle too early.

"Okay, so when do you think we should do this ladies' getaway?"

"Let's plan on two weeks from now."

"That quick?"

"Yup. That's the only time I can get off from the shelter. Fall is a busy time of year for us."

"Okay, then you make all the arrangements and call me when everything's set."

I end the call with Laney, make myself a piece of toast to go with yet another cup of coffee, and sit down to write, but my fingers wander over to Dylan's Facebook page as if on autopilot. *Here we go again*, I scold myself and shake my head, but continue scanning a few more pics and reading some of his older posts again. I notice that he sold his favorite motorcycle and has a pickup now. I guess he's given into the slower-paced lifestyle of senior life; he had a hot muscle car when I knew him.

I glance at a few of the older pictures, the ones showing him with some of the guys from the band, but I don't see any pics of Dale Perkins, who was the lead singer.

I scroll further down and a memorial post jumps into my vision. Dale passed a few years back. I sigh, remembering my friend, Tracey, who had accompanied him on a few of our double dates. I thought they would hit it off, but it didn't work out for them. Dale had led a pretty rough life.

There's a photo from an event the band did back in the spring of '76 up at Lake Geneva. Dylan looks so hot in those tight jeans and purple silk shirt.

And once again I find myself reminiscing and getting turned on. Though that's not necessarily a bad thing, I can't help but wonder why all of a sudden.

I shut down the laptop, finish my toast, and stare out the large bay window at the tall palm trees lining the backyard fence. They stand tall and straight, like centurion soldiers, keeping me here as a prisoner in my own house. Laney had said that a getaway to the beach was just what I needed, or at least, that's what she thought I needed.

# Chapter 4



*Dylan 2023*

I'm pleased with how smoothly everything's going after my last practice session. I've struck that E4 chord several times on the guitar after playing "Smoke on the Water" and "Dark Wicked Woman." three times, each time with the volume up high while chanting the words to open the time portal over and over in Latin first then in English.

"Open my heart high on the energy of the gods. Let this portal now open with a divine right."

My heart races as I'm now ready to recite this chant I devised myself:

*Jennifer, with this song*

*I play for you,*

*Know this era tried and true.*

*Only one time*

*Only one chance,*

*Take us back to the time of our romance.*

I know I got through to Jenn the other night, and it won't be long until it's all done. I mean, I could feel her, and I knew she was aroused. This spell is already working. There'll be a lot more of that once we're together again in real-time, and I'll be gone from this realm forever. Nothing will be lost here, but I want to regain what I had with her back then. It's not just my youth I've missed, but the lifestyle. Those days of traveling in the van with my buddies from venue to venue, the parties, not to mention the groupies…they all made me feel alive.

And my thoughts turn to Troy Duncan, the mastermind who was instrumental in making it all happen.

I have one more meeting with Orion's Path this weekend. I'm sure Troy will grill me on how my practice rituals are going. If only Gregg knew of my plans, I know he'd try to stop me, but I want it this way, and Troy promised never to reveal what's about to take place. I don't need anyone to go looking for me or find any sort of connection to Orion's Path.

I plan to tell Gregg I've decided to take a few weeks off to attend a rock venue in Pittsburg and then go to visit my sister. We'll be together again anyway. Once I've slipped into the other time, it'll be exactly where we left off, and he'll be none the wiser. He'll still be himself in this current earthly realm, so he won't be missed, but my shell of a body and Jenn's will be gone from 2023. At least, that's my understanding of what happens after the jump. Is it fair for me to decide for Jenn to go back? I don't care. It's all I've wanted for the past two years now.

After a quick shower, I call Gregg to see if he wants to go out for a few drinks. A divorcee for a while now, he always looks forward to our weekend outings. Our routine is simple: over to Lud's Bar for a few, then off to my studio to play a few tunes together, though this will likely be the last time that's going to happen. I have to act normally—well, as normal as possible—and keep my emotions in check. I'll just have to refrain from playing our oldies as they're now a part of the spell. They've become so much more than music and instruments—they're tools—dangerous tools, at that—and I can't risk pulling Gregg into my time warp.

# Chapter 5



Brandy calls just as I sit down at the computer, ready to start a new chapter in the final book of my romance trilogy. It's another unplanned diversion, but a good one, at least. She worries about me. I don't know why—I hardly ever leave the house. She has a lot to tell me about Brian's new job with his financial firm but not much to tell about her job as a physical therapist. Patient confidentiality is honored, even among family members.

I go on to tell her about Laney's suggestion for a ladies' getaway. No sooner have I finished than I think she's going to burst through the phone. "That's just what you need, Mom! I mean, when's the last time you got out?"

I have to think long and hard about that one. The last time I remember may have been a few years before retirement when I attended a teacher conference in West Virginia.

"Well, that's hardly getting away, if ya know what I mean," Brandy teases.

"No, it wasn't exactly something that would shake you up."

"No need to think twice about it, Mom. Time to shake things up a bit."

I take a deep breath, and my mind wanders back to the last time I was truly shaken up. I surely couldn't tell her about the thoughts I've been having about Dylan lately. After all, she'd never even heard me mention his name before. I also suppose she'd be hard-pressed to envision her mother as a groupie.

I manage to stifle a chuckle.

She's booked solid with clients, so I promise to call her later in the week to fill her in on the getaway weekend.

It's a real struggle to get back to writing. Who am I kidding? It's been months since I started the last book in the trilogy. I don't know why it's been so hard. It's not like I have any other commitments.

I decide to pack up my things and head over to Bountiful Beans, a small coffee shop close to the house. Maybe the change of scenery will do me good. I pull my hair into a high ponytail, throw on my yoga pants, and grab a light sweater. There's a brisk chill in the morning air, and it feels good. I think back to my days in Ohio when I'd get up at six and go for a run. The scent of the pines and oaks always energized me.

Those days are well behind me now.

The coffee shop isn't too crowded, it being a Sunday, and I score a table in the back, set my things down, and walk over to the counter to order a latte and a cranberry scone.

When I return to my table, I open my laptop, and Chapter Two stares me straight in the face. I go back to retrieve my order when it's ready and put in my earbuds, ready to be motivated by my 70s playlist. I take a few sips of my latte and a bite of my warm scone, ready to knock out at least a few chapters this morning. Anyway, that's the plan.

I forget I've added Grand Funk Railroad's "Heartbreaker" to my list. When it comes up in the queue, I shut down the laptop, close my eyes, and let myself get swept away in the song. It's not long before I am there, dancing at full speed to the hit as if I were back in the Regal Room when Dylan's band played the song at that very gig. I allow my body to ignore all inhibitions as I move, letting my body follow the rhythm of the song, my arms swinging, and my hips shifting from side to side. Each word has me going deeper and deeper into that night and the time I spent there with the hunky musician.

"Ma'am? Ma'am, are you all right?" a strange voice comes from beside me, shaking me out of what must have looked like a tawdry performance.

"Oh…my…God!" I find myself standing next to my table breathless, my sweater off, and the young waiter eyeing me as if I was some kind of crazed older woman either off her meds or possibly on some new ones. I guess I got carried away listening to the song. Intentionally carried away.

"I'm… fine. Just getting warmed up for my writing." I had to come up with something, seeing as how I've drawn an audience of a handful of onlookers.

He seems to buy my story but keeps a watchful eye on me as he returns to the counter, just in case I decide to bust a few moves again.

*What the hell was that about? It's just too odd.* I shake my head.

I sit here trying to regain my composure, but it's not so easy after my little performance. I close my eyes, recounting everything leading up to my dalliance, and see myself by the stage dancing away with wild abandon. And Tracey—yes, my old sidekick—is there, too. *This is no ordinary daydream seeing as how I'm fully awake in a coffee shop.* I'd never had an out-of-body experience but from what I've read on them this came pretty close.

There's no way I'm in any state to write now, so I pack up my things as quickly as I can and head out the door, minus my latte and scone.

I sit in my car for a few minutes, checking the time. It's 10 a.m.

Tracey left Poland, Ohio, and moved to Columbus shortly after she married Bill. Before that, we were thick as thieves all through high school and after. We usually went out to dinner, then headed to a local club to go dancing in the hope of meeting some hot guys.

I decide to give her a call. It'd been years since we'd seen each other, and neither of us attended the last high school reunion. I won't divulge all the woo-woo stuff going on in my head; I simply want to see how things are with her. Maybe she'll bring up something that will explain the sudden "return to yesterday" feelings I've been experiencing.

# Chapter 6


*Jennifer 2023*

It's like magic hearing Tracey's voice again. Bill has already left for work, so I catch her at a good time. After we get caught up with the usual chit-chat about health and our families, I delve gently into the past, asking her if she ever thinks of the nights spent at the clubs, dancing and dreaming about meeting guys, particularly if they were members of the band.

She's quick to respond with a "Let me tell you, girl: I wish we could bring those days back."

I sigh at the mere thought of it and remind her of the night we were locked out of my car in an area downtown that we were not supposed to be in, and some random guy had to use one of those Slim Jims to let us in. I remember my father scolding me about going to that part of town, so it wasn't as if I could have called him to rescue us. We were just seniors in high school, and our parents would have grounded us if they knew where we were.

We both got a good laugh out of that one.

Feeling more comfortable with her, I bring up the subject of Dylan and the band. "It's really strange, I tell you."

"What do you mean?" Tracey asks.

"Well, lately, I've been thinking of him. To be honest, I've been obsessing over him."

"That's not strange at all. I tell you: you've been spending too much time alone since your separation from Mark. I've got Bill and three grandkids to keep me busy, but if I were still single, I'd be obsessing, too, and you know who I mean."

She didn't have to tell me. It was Dale, the lead singer. Dylan and I had a few double dates with them. My thoughts turned to Dale, and I was at a loss for words. We both shared a moment of silence knowing he'd passed away a few years back as a result of his rough lifestyle.

I have to ask, "Do you ever go on the band's Facebook page?"

"No, and to be honest, I'm rarely on there anymore. It's changed so much, just like the times we're living in."

I have to agree with her.

I change the subject, telling her about my girlfriends' getaway with Laney to Virginia Beach.

"Hell, lady, why not the Keys? I mean, you're only a little over an hour's flight away."

"I wish my budget could afford that," I confess.

She cuts our convo short as she's expecting another call, but for the zillionth time, she asks me when I'm coming back to Ohio.

"I'm hoping maybe after the holidays." I always make promises I can't keep. I've always planned to return, but I have obligations here. My book has to be finished. I know that's a lame excuse, but it's all I can come up with at the moment. *I've made a lot of excuses lately. Was I in the early stages of becoming a hermit?*

I promise to call her when I get back to reveal all the details of my trip. And I hope there'll be at least one interesting detail worth mentioning.

We end our call, and I get an incoming call from Laney. "Hey, girl—we are all set!" Her voice is full of excitement. "We've got reservations at The Gull's Nest, beachfront, in Virginia Beach for the first week of October."

"So fast? I mean, how—"

"It was a special deal, and I had to act fast. Get online today and get your plane ticket.

This is all coming so fast. My heart races with excitement, but it's not without a bit of anxiety. I never liked being rushed, but I know Laney is trying to break me out of my rut.

"I'm not at home, but I'm headed there. I'll book as soon as I get home and send you the info."

"Get ready for five days of fun in the sun." Laney's voice is riddled with excitement.

"Maybe not too much sun with me and my fair skin," I say, examining my pale arms.

"And by the way, don't bring your laptop—no writing allowed," she orders.

"What if I get inspired?"

"Write it out on a cocktail napkin." She chuckles. "This isn't a working trip."

*I guess she expects us to spend some time in bars.*

I keep to my promise and head for my laptop as soon as I get home. Laney may have gotten a deal on the hotel, but I ended up having to pay a prime price for my plane fare.

I email her the flight info and check out the Gull's Nest website. It looks like a quaint inn, the type you'd expect to see up in New England. It's on the beachfront and has its own restaurant.

I start to feel excited, but then I think about my attire. Most of the clothes I have in my closet are casual, consisting of sportswear, jeans, shorts, and tank tops. The closet in the guest room is packed with my old teacher's wardrobe. I wonder why I never got rid of those. Guess I'll need a few dresses for our night outings.

I decide to fix a sandwich and peruse the Internet for a few new outfits. A few sexy cocktail dresses pop up. What if…?

*No way.* I let that notion go quickly by.

I realize that I'll have to email Brandy my itinerary. I know she'll be happy to see it. She's right up there with Laney when it comes to insisting that this will be just the ticket for me, but time will tell as far as I'm concerned. I tell myself that I'll write a chapter a day until I leave. I still have two weeks, and I plan to start by writing one right after dinner.

There's nothing like takeout from the local Chinese joint. I wasn't in the mood to cook…again. Seems like the non-cooking thing is becoming a trend.

I inhale my orange chicken and open the laptop, ready to pound out a few paragraphs but find myself drawn to Dylan's Facebook page.

I shake my head and wonder why, but I can't help fixating on his latest post. It's another picture of the band when they performed at Midway Park, dated August 1976. They played there at least twice a month, and Tracey and I were usually there unless something came up.

I enlarge the photo, checking out Dylan in his long-sleeved paisley shirt and bell-bottom jeans. Damn, he was smoking hot! I lean back in my chair and close my eyes, picturing him singing and performing his solo on the guitar, which he always did. It was almost as if I could hear his voice.

I snap out of my trance and stare up at the kitchen wall clock, noting that I've been sitting here for half an hour without a single word written.

*Maybe a hot shower will put me in the mood?* I reason.

Leaving the leftover food cartons on the counter, I head for the bathroom, pausing to glance in the mirror before jumping into the shower.

*You're no spring chicken anymore, Jenn—do you seriously think you're going to turn some heads in Virginia Beach?*

I examine every wrinkle closely. If only I looked the way I did forty-some years ago, I might still turn some heads when I walked into a club. There aren't many who can catch the eye of a handsome lead guitarist.

I tuck up my hair under my shower cap and jump into the steaming shower. It's not long before I realize that it's a cold one I need.

# Chapter 7

*Dylan 2023*

The night air has a sharp chill to it. I walk briskly to my pickup, crunching leaves under my boots in the parking area. I'm pleased with how tonight's session with Troy went. He was impressed with my song and the instrumental as he listened live. I took his advice to download **The Finer Pitch** app on my phone. It helps me to see if I've finally reached that high note, the one that will set off the vibrations to activate the time travel spell. It means a lot coming from the Grand Master of one of the most influential cults. It took me a full two years to finally realize it was, indeed, just that.

Again, Troy reminds me of the fact that I will be permanently stuck in the past, but as far as Jennifer is concerned, she won't be. He said it'd be hard-pressed for her to find a way back to her time given that she wouldn't have the means to do so. even if she tried.

I let those words sink in. Once she's back here I pray all will make sense to her. When she realizes this is her destiny, returning will never cross her mind.

I let the heater run for a few as I rub my hands together, warming them up. My thoughts turn to Jennifer, and it seems I don't need the heater after all. I can still feel her touch and the warmth of her skin from the last time our bodies melded together. We had such strong energy. We were like magnets. I plan to mail her the CD tomorrow. She should get it within a few days—*how long could it take for a small package to go from Ohio to Florida?* I placed a small card inside the case on which I'd written a short but enticing note, one I pray will get her to play the CD.

I need to pray. *Kidnapping is still a crime, no matter the era, and breaking and entering is enough to put me away for good. Then again, I reason, no one will be able to find me and convict me in this era.* The only two people who know about my plan are Troy and me. I haven't even told Gregg, which is hard because we've shared so much over the years. It's going to be difficult to act normal when I see him tomorrow night when we plan to meet at Lud's for a few drinks.

I pull off US 62 and into the Fed-Ex parking lot to send off the package. The clerk asks me about the contents, and I stifle a chuckle, thinking about what he might do if I tell him it's an enchanted CD that will open a time portal.

The balding middle-aged man smiles as I pay him my twenty-five dollars to overnight it.

Traffic is light on the way home. I stop at The Wicked Wok to grab some takeout for dinner. I scoped out the old abandoned club again last night and pretty much know every single inch of that building. I even have a point of entry planned. Everything on my end is done. The rest is up to Jennifer. It'll be a rough next couple of days, waiting to see if she'll listen to the CD. Only time will tell.

I have nothing to pack but three small items I've saved from the seventies. I have my old guitar pick, a faded ticket from the Regal Room, and a Polaroid of Jenn and me, taken in one of those old-time photo booths at Midway Park.

According to Troy, everything will still be as it was back in '76. I'll have to leave my phone, wallet, and anything that belongs in this era at home. I plan to leave the pickup in Fisker's market's backlot.
I beat Gregg to Lud's and order a beer. The smell of greasy, grilled burgers fills the air as I take a seat on the worn red leather barstool, gazing around at all the old photos hanging behind the bar. They were taken mostly in the sixties through to the eighties. There are a few of celebs, as well, but most are icons from Youngstown in an era when the city was run by the mob. I won't deny that a close friend's father played a huge role in the mob at the time, and I never turned down any of the items he claimed had "fallen off the truck."

A tap on my shoulder signals Gregg's arrival, followed by our usual handshake. His hands are dry and rough, which matches the skin on his face. He had a rough life during our band years and after. I know his health is poor, but he keeps up a good front.

He takes a seat next to me and tightens the thin leather band securing his long, grey ponytail. "See ya beat me again, you old dog!" Gregg says as he signals the bartender.

"Guess I did, old buddy. You're looking happy tonight. Got a hot date or something?"

"I should be so lucky. No, actually, I just got an email from a new music promoter in Cleveland. Seems he's looking to put together a venue in the spring, and he wants some of the older local bands to be featured, including ours. I just may drive down there and check it out."

I have to search for words here. "Well, now, that *is* something to celebrate," I answer back, thinking that I most likely won't be there, and neither will Dale, our lead singer, for that matter.

The bartender slides a beer over to Gregg, and I mention that this one's on me.

A few middle-aged blondes walk by, and Gregg's eyes track them as they head over to a booth a few feet away. I shake my head and slap him lightly on the shoulder.

"I remember the days when we had all the girls just waiting for us to give them some attention if ya know what I mean," Gregg says.

I sigh. *If he only knew I'm going to be with one of those girls soon.*

I nod my head in response to his statement. "Yes, those were the days, my friend."

Gregg prattles on about the details of the upcoming venue, and I pretend to give him my full attention.

I finish my second beer and decline another, knowing I'll have to drive home. Gregg informs me that he's taking an Uber, and he orders another. He tells me of his tentative plan to contact the other guys, including Bob Mazare, who was a backup singer when Dale missed a few performances due to illness.

I glance at my watch, noting that it's almost midnight. I want to make one more run by the old building that used to house the Regal

Room, so I tell Gregg I'll be in touch, knowing damn well I'll be in touch with him in a bygone era soon, and encourage him to go over to buy those blondes a drink.

A wave of sadness falls over me as I pull out of the gravel parking lot and onto the highway. It'll probably be the last time I'll see him and the other guys in the band in this realm, but I have to focus on channeling my thoughts on what lies ahead of me. One vision of Jennifer is all it takes to snap my attention back to my mission, and my body reacts the way it always does when I think of her.

In just a few days, I'll be breaking into the Regal Room and ready to journey back to a place I know I belong.

# Chapter 8



*Jennifer 2023*

I barely make it to the kitchen to make some breakfast before Laney calls me. "Hey, lady," she says, "didn't mean to wake you, but—"

"But what?" With a call that early, I fear she has some bad news.

"I hate to put a dampener on things, but I can't make it to our girls' getaway. I have to watch my grandson. My daughter has to go out of town on business."

"No worries," I say, actually relieved to have an excuse not to go. I need to get my book done.

"I'm so sorry, my friend. I promise to make it up to you. I haven't canceled the reservation at the resort yet. I was waiting to see if you wanted to go."

"Uggh … I don't think so. You have nothing to apologize about. I'm going to call the airlines this morning and see if I can get a refund, although it's most unlikely."

"Wait a minute—you should go. It's just the thing you need. You know how much you've been talking about this book you have to finish—it'll be a nice change of environment, the perfect place to find some inspiration."

I sigh. "I don't think I want to go alone. I'm not the type to do something like that," I say, pouring myself a cup of tea.

"There's always time to start, my dear. You might be pleasantly surprised."

I take a sip of coffee and try to internalize her words. "I'm not sure. Maybe I'll think about it."

"Well, take my advice and spend the day packing—you leave next week."

We end the call. I walk over to the bay window and glance out at the back deck and the rose bushes that border it that are in desperate need of some pruning. *It would be a nice change of scenery. Maybe Laney is right.*

My head spins with all the things I'll need to do if I decide to go. I glance at the laptop on the kitchen table, and that somehow helps me make the decision.

Right after breakfast, I call Brandy to let her know, and she's ecstatic for me. I tell her I don't care if she tells her father as I'm surely not about to call him.

I head back into the bedroom to take inventory of the clothes I might take. I finally broke down and ordered two new dresses online, and they should arrive this week. One is a knee-length, red cocktail dress, and the other is an off-the-shoulder black dress.

Lying on the beach and evenings writing in my suite have started to sound quite appealing. I don't know if I'll be brave enough to venture out to the clubs Laney mentioned. Once again, my mind races back to the nights Tracey and I went from club to club, following Ablaze to all of their gigs. I long for those times to return. Lately, I've been dwelling on those times in excess.

I call Laney back to let her know I'm going it alone. Just taking that step makes me feel more confident.

It's already mid-week. My anticipation only grows as the weekend comes closer. I have to make sure everything is ready for the trip. I have a checklist; teachers always have a checklist. As they say, "Once a teacher, always a teacher."

I call my daughter and then confirm the reservations at the resort. I ask my widowed neighbor, DeeDee, to keep an eye on the house, and if any packages come to the door, to please keep them at her house. She's in her late seventies but still sharp as a tack. I managed to check on her frequently, as she does me. We both live alone and know the comfort of having a friend to rely on.

Next week, I'll get my hair done. I have the inkling to get some highlights this time. Why not?

Both of the dresses I ordered came today. I got lucky this time with my online order. Both of them fit and look classy. *And where did I think I would wear these?*

I snap a few pics of me in them to shoot off to Laney. Her text comes back quickly: *You look sexy! Snag a guy or two.*

I have to chuckle. She makes me think I'm only going there to pick up a hot date. *That's a long shot. One I wouldn't bet on.*

I triple-check everything the next week. Tomorrow, I can check in online and print out my boarding pass. I'll take an Uber to Tampa International Airport on Saturday morning.

Hearing the sound of an engine running, I glance out the window to see a UPS truck and the driver approaching with a large envelope that he leaves on my front porch though I can't recall ordering anything. I open the door to fetch the thick, manilla envelope.

*Hmm, what could it be?*

I slice it open with a small knife to find a small CD inside, along with a card. *What in the world—*

I read the card:

***Jennifer,***

***I was thinking of you recently and thought you might want to listen to this again. After all, it was your favorite song. It's been a long time.***

***I hope it brings back some great memories.***

***Dylan***

I stand there, dumbfounded, and pull out the CD. It has "Play Me" written on it.

*Why would he send this to me now, after all these years?* I think about how odd it all is, given that I've been fixated on him lately. *I mean, does he know? How could he? Does he have a spy peeking in my windows?* The only people I told were Laney and Tracey, and Tracey knows our backstory.

I place the CD on my desk next to my older computer, the one with the CD player, planning to listen to it later, after my shower. *Maybe it will relax me or make me fantasize about him again.*

# Chapter 9



Though it's nearing midnight, I drive by the old Regal Room building to scope it out one more time. I have to have this down to the very minute. I plan to break in tomorrow, Friday night. I figure Jenn will most likely have listened to the CD by then, and it will be the perfect time to set the intention.

Not wanting to be conspicuous, I park the truck in the parking lot of the old Fisker's Food Market across the street and notice an older blue SUV parked in the front lot.

*What the hell?*

I sneak around to the back, not wanting to be noticed, where I see a tall, elderly man in a security uniform. *Now, that's unexpected. Now, what?* I need to come up with a plan…and fast. I walk over to the fenced-in area where there's an entrance gate and call out to him. He shines his flashlight on me and comes over. "This is private property, sir. What business do you have here?"

The words flow from my mouth like silk. "I once played here with my band, Ablaze, many years ago. I only want to take a look around again. You know, for old time's sake."

To my surprise, he buys my excuse. "I've heard of your band. I didn't grow up in this area, but I've heard others speak about it. Heard you guys almost went big time. Can't blame you for wanting to relive a few memories. I've been there myself."

He opens the gate to let me pass and walks me over to the back door. I wait for him to unlock the door, thinking how perfect it would be if I could simply get his key, but that won't happen unless I knock him out and steal it. If he's here tomorrow night, I'll have to do whatever needs to be done. Nothing's gonna stop me from claiming my destiny.

I take the small flashlight out of my pocket and walk through the main entrance. He looks at me and says, "I see you've come prepared. Take your time. I'll be out back here when you're done. Enjoy the memories."

With the beam of my flashlight as my guide, I step into the vast expanse of the once-thriving club. The air hangs heavily with the weight of memories. The old bar is an island of nostalgia amidst an empty sea. The stage, a relic of forgotten performances, beckons me.

A stack of weathered red leather and chrome chairs rests in the back corner, a testament to the countless conversations and laughter that once filled the space. The green, ball-chain-style lamps that once illuminated the bar area are now shrouded in cobwebs as if time itself has spun a web around them to protect their secrets.

The musty scent filling my nostrils is a reminder that the past never truly fades away. It speaks of countless nights of revelry and shared dreams, but it's not just the scent that grips me—it's the palpable sense of history clinging to every surface, hiding in every crack of the worn-out floorboards.

I climb onto the weathered stage and find my place on its edge, the darkness wrapping around me like a comfortable shroud. I close my eyes and allow the weight of the years to settle upon me. Chills race down my spine, but it's a welcome sensation. It's as though the spirits of the past are reaching out, acknowledging my presence. It's without a doubt I've left my imprint here.

Abandoned places are more than just dilapidated structures—they're vessels of time, echoes of moments both good and bad. As I sit here enveloped by the darkness, those echoes reverberate through my very being.

And soon Jenn and I are poised to relive that time—that is if everything goes according to plan.

I walk out to the back entrance, close the door behind me, and call for the guard, who heads over my way.

"All done?"

"Yes, sir. Thank you for letting me in. You've made an old man happy tonight."

"It was my pleasure," he replies as he locks up the back door.

I have to ask one more question. "So, how long have you been working here?"

"Not long. The owners hired me shortly after there was some vandalism."

"Any cameras?" I pry. *I know I didn't see any in the club.*

"No need. The owner plans to bulldoze this place and sell the land to a company that plans to build a smoke shop. I'm sure there will be cameras set up for the new place along with an alarm system."

That last statement shakes me. Guess I'm doing this just in time. Doesn't matter if they tear it down because I'll be locked away in the past. My only worry now is how I'll deal with the guard tomorrow.

I thank the friendly guard again and head over to sit in my pickup. The guy looks as if I can take him. I'll need to knock him out to take his key. By the time he recovers, I should be long gone. The only thing he'll find in there is the same old dark, dusty club.

Surely, there will be clues, such as my pickup across the street, which will prompt the cops to locate my address as they search for the owner. Hope they have a fun run chasing a ghost.

# Chapter 10



*Dylan 2023*

I phoned Troy late last night, and he offered me an injectable vial of Midazolam, which is primarily used for patients undergoing medical procedures. It causes severe drowsiness and can even prevent one from remembering events before the injection. Troy is a sheer genius, I have to say. I plan on driving over there shortly after lunch.

My mind races with thoughts of seeing Jenn again, but subtle shades of doubt sweep in, clouding my excitement. *What if this doesn't work? What if she doesn't listen to the CD? I won't be able to go back and will most likely be arrested for attempting to murder the night guard.* I have to recite the chant three times while in the Regal Room and meditate while holding the guitar pick, the old ticket, and the photo of Jenn and me.

It's good to see Troy again, though it'll most likely be the last time I'll see him, at least, in this realm. He answers the door wearing his thick, black-framed glasses and holds an astronomy book in his hand. I follow him into the basement of his home, where he has a small but impressive makeshift lab. He whispers to me, and I don't know why, as I assume we are the only people here. I did hear rumors of him having a bodyguard. He's lived alone for most of his life, and I know he has no sessions scheduled for tonight.

He hands me a small plastic container sealed in bubble wrap. "You've got to keep this chilled and use it within an hour once you take it out of the fridge or cooler if that's what you are using."

I hold his gaze, listening intently to his directions, waiting until he's done before I ask what I'm afraid of. "What, exactly, are the side effects here?"

He tells me one can expect things such as a headache, vomiting, seizures, and difficulty breathing, but if one is in good health, they should come to in a few hours with nothing more than a bad headache, comparable to having a hangover. The trouble is, I don't know if the guy has any health issues. He looked as if he was in his mid to late seventies. I didn't have time to explore his past medical history, and at this point, my only concern is getting back to the seventies.

Troy gives me a strong handshake, and I thank him for all he's done. Without him, none of this would even be possible. I've gained his trust and know none of our secret meetings would ever be divulged. He's managed to keep Orion's Path a secret for the past ten years, and he wouldn't risk compromising the organization.

I don't have much of an appetite. My stomach's cramping with nerves coupled with excitement. I heat up a frozen burrito and manage to eat it while I gather all the necessary items. I have a small black backpack where I store the guitar pick, the note with the chant, the photo, and of course, a small flashlight. I decide to leave my wallet and my phone at home—I remember Troy saying I can't take anything in with me that might link me to this timeline.

I glance down at my jeans, and yeah, they're Levi's, but the brand's been around forever, so I guess it's all good. I have a small collection of authentic, vintage rock and roll T-shirts I purchased on eBay and pull on the black Allman Brothers one.

After woofing down the last of my burrito, I grab the injectable, pop it into a small cooler, and head for my truck. It's only a half-hour's drive into Youngstown. With my hand still on the doorknob, I look back at my modest ranch home one more time and sigh. *Thanks for the memories.*

It's nearing midnight when I pull into Fisker's Market's rear parking lot, get out of the truck, sling the backpack over my right shoulder, and head across the street. There's no sign of the guard, but I know he's there as his blue SUV is in the lot.

I walk briskly toward the back entrance gate. There's a padlock on it with a heavy chain, and still no sight of the guard. *Hmm…maybe the old man's sleeping somewhere.*

*I need that damn key!*

I take a chance and walk over to his SUV to see if he's there. As I near the vehicle, I make out the figure of a man slumped over the steering wheel. *Yup. Just as I thought. He's asleep.*

I rap on the window, and he jolts out of his slumber and rolls down the window, surprised to see me.

"I'm sorry to bother you again, but I need to get one more picture of the joint if you'll allow me to do so," I say, praying he'll fall for it.

He rubs his eyes and opens the driver's side door. "You again? Guess you can't stay away." He motions for me to follow him over to the back gate. My heart races, knowing that at any moment, I'll need to knock him down and inject him with the juicy cocktail Troy whipped up.

I'm right behind him as he opens the back door and motions for me to step inside. When I turn to thank him, we lock eyes. I put one hand on his shoulder and throw him down onto the pavement.

He shouts, but I straddle his hips, reach for the needle, and inject it into his left thigh. Troy said it would be the safest and easiest way. I watch him struggle as he tries to push me off, yelling for help, but I stay put long enough for the meds to take effect.

When I'm sure he's out like a light, I drag his limp body back to his SUV and place him in the backseat. Most likely, he'll wake up without realizing what happened to him. *I should be so lucky.*

I race over to the unlocked door, take my items out of my backpack, and put them in my pocket, leaving my backpack at the door. Time is of the essence here and I need to get onto that stage. I pull out my flashlight to illuminate my way to the main hall. When I leap onto the stage, I place my items out in front of me and assume the Lotus position on the floor. Deep breathing and meditation come easily for me; they have for the past two years, ever since I've been attending Orion's Path.

I don't need to look at the chant in my notes as I've memorized it. I've practically lived it for the past year. I close my eyes and recite:

*Jennifer, with this song*
*I play for you,*
*Know this era tried and true*
*Only one time*
*Only one chance,*
*Take us back to the time of our romance.*

# Chapter 11



I take a deep breath and close the large purple suitcase, the one I plan to check. My carry-on is all ready to go. I just need to throw in some last-minute makeup items along with my laptop, which I'll do in the morning after I get dressed. I think about how much I'll miss Laney on this trip. It won't be the same without her. My boarding pass is already printed, and I have secured my Uber driver to arrive at 8 a.m. I figure I should be in Virginia Beach around 11:30 tomorrow morning—it's only a two-hour flight into Norfolk Airport.

I'm a bit antsy about my trip and decide to relax with a glass of wine. While I wait, I stare at the CD and card Dylan sent. I'm not sure if I can listen to it now. I read the words "Play Me" and wonder what might be recorded on it. When I can no longer ignore my curiosity, I head over to my office to retrieve my old computer, the one with the CD player installed, and bring it into the living room. Just what is this man up to?

There is some static at first, but then I hear that song playing, the same song that made me fall in love with Dylan: "Dark Wicked Woman." I listen, swaying back and forth as I do, getting lost in the lyrics. The music seems to get louder and louder as the song plays on, though I haven't touched the volume.

My wine still sits on the coffee table, but I've lost interest in it. All I want is to dance, hard and wild.

When the music stops, a voice comes on—it's Dylan! I stop dancing and listen to the words he speaks to me.

I start to feel a bit lightheaded, so I take a seat on the sofa.

Dylan continues to recite the same short poem again and again.

I'm glad I'm sitting because the lightheadedness has turned into full-blown vertigo. I faintly hear the wall clock strike midnight before my ears start to ring so loud it drowns out the sound of Dylan's voice.

I lie back down on the sofa, and everything goes black.

My head is pounding when I come to. I steady myself and try to pull myself from the floor.

I look down, and it's not my floor!

*What the hell?*

I'm lying on an old black and white tiled floor in a large restroom stall. I try to stand, but I am still woozy. I hold onto the side wall for support.

The words on the stall door, which are fuzzy and black, come slowly into focus: "For a good time, call Babs."

*This has to be a dream! What was in that wine?*

*Wait a minute…I didn't drink the wine. The last I remember, I was dancing to a song. Must've gotten dizzy and passed out.*

I manage to regain my stance, and when I'm steady enough, I open the stall door. The restroom is dimly lit, but it looks vaguely familiar, with the shiny black sinks and oval mirrors, with decorative ivy plants painted around the rims.

*What. The. Fuck?*

*I know this place. I'm in the restroom of the old Regal Room Club!*

*It can't be!*

I glance in the mirror to see that I look the same as I did some forty-five years ago. I look closer to examine my fair skin dotted with freckles and my silky, long strawberry-blonde hair. And my top! I remember this top! Mom made the yellow lace halter top for me.

I run my hand over my stomach—it's flat. Flat! *What kind of magic is this?* I turn to stare at the door, waiting for someone to come in and rescue me from this nightmare.

*Was I drugged?*

I hear many voices outside the door, so I splash cold water on my face and decide to venture out.

What I see stuns me. Yup, I'm in the Regal Room, and it's just as I remember it back in the day. I freeze, taking it all in.

The bar is hopping, the tables are packed with people, and someone is calling my name.

*No!*

*No way!*

*No. Fucking. Way.*

I see Tracey Blaznick standing up and waving me over to a table by the front of the stage. I make my way over to the table and take a seat, still lightheaded.

Tracey grabs my hand and helps me to a chair. "You look as if you've seen a ghost."

I search for words, trying not to look her in the eye. I'm too busy checking out the stage, where a band has set up their equipment…and there it is, that familiar logo on the drums: *Ablaze!*

I'm lightheaded again. I feel as though I'm about to vomit.

Tracey orders me a drink, a rum and Coke. It was my go-to drink every time we went out.

I gulp half of it down, slam the glass on the tabletop, look her in the eye, and prepare to ask her a stupid question. It's one I should have thought more about before opening my mouth.

"How did I get here?"

She looks at me quizzically. "Now I'm really worried about you. Did you fall and hit your head in there?"

I try to factor all of this out. *Maybe I fell while dancing? Maybe I died, and this is heaven, and if so, heaven is a nightclub.*

*Uggh!*

I shake my head, finish my drink, and order another.

Tracey hugs me tightly and tells me the band is about to play their second session. She whispers in my ear that she knows I've had the hots for the lead guitarist, and when the music starts, we are going to go out on the floor and bust our best moves.

The colored lights flash over the stage, and the band members come out and head for their instruments. Dale settles out front, wearing a blue glitter shirt, his long blond hair hanging halfway over his face, and I realize I'm staring at a dead man. Gregg takes a seat at the drums. Then, I see Dylan pick up his guitar and play around, tuning it up. *God, he's so hot!* His jeans are so tight, and his usual black T-shirt is molded to his strong, muscular body.

The band starts to play. Tracey tugs on my arm and leads me to the dance floor. I'm still numb. I figure I must be caught in some kind of time warp or parallel universe.

Their first number is Deep Purple's "Smoke on the Water." I remember that one so well. I go along with Tracey, figuring I might as well enjoy it. What have I got to lose? I might as well enjoy this dream.

I don't want to look at Dylan, but I know I will—it's destiny. It's already happened in the past.

I catch him staring at me, and I play it to the hilt, giving him just what he wants—to watch my body as I move wildly to the music.

He winks at me, and I turn to see Tracey smile back at me. *Oh, this is too damn freaky!*

I wonder if this will play out just as it did some forty-five years ago.

# Chapter 12



*Jennifer*

After the sixth song, the band is ready to take its last break of the evening. Tracey pulls my arm. "Look—he's headed straight for our table!"

I can't utter even a single word. My eyes are focused on the hunky guitar player with the skin-tight jeans and wispy, long shag cut. My heart leaps when he touches my shoulder. "Can I buy you a drink?" he asks.

I come out of my semi-coma to give him an answer, stand, and follow him to the bar without turning back to look at my friend. He leads me over to sit on one of the red vinyl stools and motions for the bartender. "What would you like?"

Two simple words come out of my mouth: "rum and Coke."

He orders a White Russian.

The words "White Russian" ring a bell in my head, and I remember that was his drink of choice.

He sits on the stool next to me, and I flash him a smile. "I've been wanting to meet you. Been watching you dance for some time now."

"Really? I love to dance."

"I take it you know that my girlfriend and I follow your band."

"It's hard not to notice," he says, holding my gaze with his.

He has the most hypnotic hazel eyes ever. The subtle green lights hanging above the bar seem to illuminate them, but that's not what attracts me to him. It's his voice and the way he moves on that stage. I did have a thing for musicians, but he is special. He's got some good energy—or should I say good sexual energy?

The bartender slides our drinks across the shiny mahogany counter, and I grab the frosty glass and give it a slight stir. I can't take a sip until he goes first. I thank him, and he begins to strike up a conversation. I know exactly where this is going. Let's see if it ends where I remember.

He asks me where I'm from and all the pertinent details, smiling when I tell him I'm a local Struthers girl—the band did have quite a few groupies from the area. I go on to tell him I've recently graduated from Youngstown State University and hope to begin teaching soon, or at least substitute teaching.

He tells me he graduated from North Central High, has no plans to attend college, and wants to work on his music career. He tells me the band has a road tour coming up this winter.

The drummer comes by and taps him on the shoulder. "Gotta go, man. One more set to go for the evening."

Dylan takes the last sip of his drink and asks for my number. I fish a pen out of my fringed suede bag and write it on the cocktail napkin without having to even think about it. I get that odd feeling again, and the hairs stand up on the back of my neck.

*How did I do that? How did I remember my old home number?*

Dylan tucks the napkin in his back jeans pocket and whispers in my ear, "I'll call you soon."

And I know he will. Like this weekend. He'll ask me to accompany him and the band to Midway Park, where they will play at an outdoor venue.

I carry my drink over to the table where Tracey is waiting to hear all the details.

We dance to a few more songs, and she reminds me that she'd like to be home before one. She doesn't leave without voicing her concern over the state of my well-being. "You sure you're okay to drive? I mean, you did have a dizzy spell in the restroom."

I hadn't thought about that. I have to drive home.

*Is my car out in the parking lot? I sure as hell can't call an Uber.*

I bid her goodnight, hug her, and sit for a few more minutes at our table, trying to digest everything.

It's not every day you get to travel back to your past.

* * *

I head out into the parking lot, assuming my old 1972 Roadrunner is there, the bronze one with the two large black racing stripes down the hood.

The lot is still pretty crowded, so I walk its length like a lost soul, unsure of what I'm looking for. As I approach the end of the lot by the side road, I see it, my old Roadrunner. My heart skips a beat, and I freeze at the sight.

I reach into my bag, searching for the key. There won't be a fob—they had nothing like that back then, at least, not that I know of.

The shiny metal key unlocks the door, and I slip into the smooth black leather seats. I stare at the large pistol shifter in the center—*to think I used to drive this thing! Do I even remember how to shift?*

I start the old car and pull out of the lot, headed onto Youngstown Poland Road toward Allen Street. Funny how I know the way home. Not so funny when I consider that I've lived in that house for seventeen years.

When I pull up to park in the driveway of the two-story, brick, colonial-style house, I sit there, staring up at my old bedroom window on the second floor. *Is it still pink and green? Is the thick pink shag carpet still there? Is my ivy plant still thriving as it hangs in the macramé hanger I made?*

*Wait—are Mom and Dad sleeping in their bedroom…alive?*

I pinch myself. This has to be a dream. Either that or I've died. Maybe I had slipped down some wormhole?

I enter the house and step into the kitchen. The old rooster nightlight by the sink illuminates the seventies-style bronze appliances and the old country wallpaper. Everything is dark, so I assume Mom and Dad are, indeed, up in bed.

As I climb the stairs, a chill runs up my spine, and my pulse pounds in my ears. *Should I wake them to ask what's happening? Should I tell them? Would they even believe me?*

I pass by Joe's room. The door is open, and his bed is still made. I figure he's still out, partying with his friends.

I pad down the hallway and make a dead stop right in front of Mom and Dad's bedroom. I feel as if I can't breathe.

The door is open, so I walk in. Mom hears me and sits up in bed as I come around to her side of the bed. It's good the room is dark so she won't notice the pallor of my skin.

*How is it that I'm standing here with two people who passed away ten years ago?*

"Glad you made it home, hon," she whispers so as not to wake Dad, who is asleep beside her.

"Y . . . yes." I kiss her softly and run my hands over her bob-length silver hair, smelling the Chantilly lace powder she always used. I hold back the tears and tell myself this is not the time for a breakdown.

"I had a good time. I'll tell you all about it in the morning. Get some sleep."

I head for my room and click on the wall switch, which turns on the small lamp on my nightstand with the pink floral shade. I throw my jacket and purse on the bed. Out of habit, I look in my bag, searching for my phone, but I guess certain things can't travel with you to a different time.

I pull open the wooden sliding door to my closet, and there they are, just as I remember, all the hallmark pieces of a classic seventies-style wardrobe: hip-hugger jeans, block-printed dresses, two maxi coats, and a few miniskirts. I close the door and take a deep breath. My clock on the nightstand reads 1:30 a.m. I'm too tired at this point to figure any of this out, so I turn down my fluffy, floral-printed comforter and slip into bed.

*Perhaps things will be back to normal when I wake up tomorrow.*

# Chapter 13



*Dylan 1976*

Gregg is the last one to grab his coat from the dressing room wardrobe. He walks over to the small sofa where I am lying and sits on the edge. "You okay, man? Gotta watch your liquor when we have a gig."

I sit up, still a bit dizzy, but it fades quickly. "I'm fine. Just tired. Didn't get much sleep last night." *Actually, I was too busy assaulting an old man, breaking and entering this club, and enacting a spell to get myself and my old girlfriend back together. Oh, if he only knew the truth.*

"I know we drove separately, but we can drive back home together?" Gregg says.

"Honestly, I'm just going to stay here a few and go over the schedule for the next few weeks," I lie.

"Does seeing that hot blonde have a slot in your schedule?" he pries.

I turn and smile at him. "You know me well, Gregg. I'll see ya back at the apartment soon."

Once Gregg leaves, I lie back down. It's been quite a night. I guess seeing Jenn again really took everything out of me. I can't believe I pulled it off! Fuck! The spell worked! I'm back, and so is Jenn. I pull out the note and picture from my pocket. She looks just like I remember her. I wanted to take her right there on that dance floor. She still had that lean body and that angelic-looking face.

I take a few deep breaths. How will I ever control myself?

I need to play this out, take things slow. I'm sure she's trying to sort things out now, figuring out how the hell she got back here. She'll never guess it was all my doing. I don't even care, just as long as we're together.

I realize I need to destroy the picture as it hasn't happened yet. I also have to destroy the note. Lord help me if someone got a hold of them. These things are evidence.

I stand and walk over to the dressing table, take a seat, and look in the mirror. The old shag haircut hasn't seemed to move, even with my prancing all over that stage tonight. I was back in my jam, the place I've always wanted to be. It's funny how one can pass through time and come out without a single scratch. I examine the rest of my body, making sure it's all in place.

I run my hands down my jeans. Yep, the old boy's still there, and yearning to get between Jenn's firm thighs.

Guess by now the old 2023 guard should be coming to, and the police have been called, but that doesn't concern me now that I'm no longer there.

My work is cut out for me here. I need to make sure Jenn is content and doesn't try to find her way back. I think about what Troy said, that it would be almost impossible for her to find a way back, *but what if she finds out? Then again, how could she?* My head starts to pound—Troy forgot to mention that one of the side effects would be a bad headache.

I walk over to the bar area where the bartender is closing up shop for the night. Old Jack looks just as I remember him as well. His untamed beard and wire-rimmed glasses always reminded me of some old character from a Western movie. His pants were held up with those red suspenders that were his trademark. I remember all the late-night talks we had back then about his divorce. Of course, that won't happen for a few months now. Drinks were always on the house for the band, just one of the perks I always enjoyed, but I knew he didn't have any coffee, and I didn't need another drink.

He tells me the band sounded good tonight as he pats me on the back.

The lights go out in the club as I head out the exit door for the car with only one thing on my mind: We did it, Jenn. We made it happen. You just have to trust fate.

# Chapter 14

*Jennifer*

I rub my eyes, trying to clear the crust that has settled in the corners overnight.

*Damn it—I didn't remove my eye makeup last night.*

*Last night.*

*Last night!*

*What the hell happened?*

Daylight peeks through the curtains, and I sit up, focusing on my front bedroom window that faces the Dalman's house across the street. *I'm still stuck in this dream. I'm supposed to be on my way to Virginia Beach.*

My head throbs as I rub my temples. The clock reads 8 a.m. I know where I am, but I don't even know what day it is or what month or year, for that matter. *This is beyond insane!*

Familiar voices pervade my madness as I walk out into the hall, listening. It's Mom's voice, speaking to Dad. I shake my head and move past Joe's room. The door is closed. He must be asleep. Most likely had some decent partying with his buddies last night.

I turn to head back to my room and open the closet to find my old, pink terrycloth robe in the back. I throw it on and brace myself for whatever I might encounter when I go downstairs, take in a deep breath, and pray to God for strength to get through this.

Mom greets me with a hug right after she pours Dad a cup of coffee. She's wearing her usual button-down print housecoat, the one I remember so vividly growing up. "Hope we didn't wake you. We tried to be quiet."

Dad breaks out in a big smile as I walk over to him. I'm trying to hold back the tears as best I can, but it's a struggle seeing the people I'd lost to cancer ten years ago.

52

Dad asks about my night as I hug him. He's got the newspaper on the table. Knowing him, he'll read it a few times over throughout the day. I glance at it, noticing the date: Saturday, 1976.

I sit in my usual spot and tell him it was great. He's still as handsome as ever. His silver hair and pale blue eyes were like his trademark, one people tended to remember. His appearance complimented Mom's so well, with her silver hair and deep brown eyes.

Mom asks if I've met anyone special, as she always does. I know she was genuinely concerned—now that I was out of college, the time was right for choosing a husband, and being Italian, I guess it was in her nature.

She takes out a mug from the cupboard and pours me a cup of coffee. My heart skips a beat when I see the mug. It's the green one she bought for me in Volant, PA, the one with the Amish buggy on it. We used to go there on weekends to shop. We both enjoyed all the little shops and unique crafts. It was like our special mother-and-daughter thing.

"Something wrong, Jenn?" she asks when she sets the mug on the table.

I force myself to snap out of my trance. "No, I'm just sleepy. I need this coffee."

She goes on to tell me that Joe's still in bed, and she and Dad are planning to go to the Italian market today. She asks if I would like anything special. I would love to go, but I need to figure out this ongoing nightmare. I tell her I have plans to work on my paperwork to substitute teach for our local school district, which brings a wide smile to her face. She always wanted me to be a teacher and was proud I'm finally working on bringing that dream to fruition.

I grab a fresh cheese Danish from the plate on the table and devour it as if I haven't eaten in days. I guess going insane makes you hungry, especially for sweets.

When I'm done, I excuse myself to shower and get dressed. I'm thankful Joe is still sleeping. I don't think I could endure seeing him in his early twenties—I haven't seen him since he moved to Arizona, and it's been years; he's sixty-three in my time.

The next throwback is when I open the bathroom cabinet to find my old brand of shampoo and conditioner that they don't make anymore, in my time. I open the cap and bring it to my nose. The herbal scent provides a rush to my brain, and a good one, at that. Seems as if we remember scents as well as we do actual memories.

I run the water in the shower and hop in, taking my time to reflect on all of this.

As I suds up with the strawberry shower gel, my thoughts turn to Dylan and last night. Damn, he looked so good. That chemistry we always had got to me yet again. I wonder if he'll call me today. If my memories serve me right, he did phone me the day after I met him.

I let my hand travel down to my sweet spot which begs for attention caused by all the visuals of Dylan last night that still rack my brain and my body. I take care of that issue. Feeling sated, I need to focus on the matter at hand.

Laney.

I think of Laney. She lives here in Youngstown, but we don't meet until we teach school together in the early eighties. If I try to contact her, she won't even know who I am, and there's no way she'll buy my story. I could call Tracey and try to explain to her, but she'll think I'm crazy as well. Still, she's my best friend and my only hope, so I have to give it a shot.

I rush back to my room, close the door, and call Tracey using the old pink princess phone on my nightstand. She answers on the third ring, but I decide this isn't a conversation to be done over the phone, so I ask her if she can meet me for lunch at Marcone's Italian Café.

After we end our call, I think about money for lunch, so I ransack my old red faux leather wallet to find a couple of tens. There are no credit cards. I didn't have any yet. I did, however, have a checking account at the local bank along with a checkbook I could access as backup.

I need a computer, and I need it fast. I need my iPhone! Trying to think rationally, I decide to visit the local library, which is the next best thing.

I pull on a pair of hip-hugger jeans and a long-sleeve Henley top, hoping the weather won't be too chilly.

After making an excuse to leave early, I kiss Mom and Dad goodbye and head out for the library, which is twenty minutes away by car. Luckily, Joe's still asleep. I'll deal with him later. I wonder if this isn't a dream after all, but some Supernatural Time Glitch. *What if people start looking for me in my time? Will Brandy call me? What about Mark?*

No, Mark wouldn't, but Brandy would most likely call the police, and Laney expected a call from me when I got to Virginia Beach. I think about calling her but that won't end well either.

My pulse quickens the moment I open the door to the driver's side of my old Road Runner. *What was with me and muscle cars?* I shake my head, start the engine, and have to struggle with the damn pistol shifter once again.

I hope the library will have the information I need. I'm sure there are books in there on time travel, wormholes, and the like. *Did people even believe in this stuff back then?* I know I wasn't sure about them even in my time until I had to do some research on wormholes for one of the books I had to edit for a friend a few years back, so I know there are ways to travel between realms as a few had mentioned in complicated scientific terms.

Whatever the reason, I have Tracey as a backup, and I'm looking forward to meeting her for lunch. I pray she doesn't lose her appetite when she hears what I'm about to tell her.

# Chapter 15

What a head trip it is as I pull into the Smithtown Library. It brings back so many memories of my days spent here when I was in high school and college. I wasn't even sure the place would still be there, and I don't know why when every other place here is exactly where it was back in '76.

I pull into the back parking lot and wonder if I even have a library card. I tear my wallet apart again and find one tucked in the back of one of the folds. I sit for a moment gazing at my picture—it must have been taken during freshman year. I look so much younger. I'm sure the librarian will want me to renew this but I don't have the time. Then again, I'm simply here to look into some books, not check them out, and I know there's a microfiche down in the basement where I spent hours during my senior year at YSU. There should be copies of old magazines and news articles down there.

I stop by the front desk, where a middle-aged lady with short, curly blonde hair greets me. I tell her I'm here for research and to inquire about microfiche usage. She directs me to the card catalog and tells me I can find whatever else I need in the basement, as if I didn't already know that.

*This is turning out to be the weirdest case of deja vu ever.*

There are a few books on time travel and wormholes, and I pull them off the shelves and hunt for a secluded table in the back, one away from all the families there with their little ones. I don't need the distraction. I also don't want any of the locals to recognize me. I don't know why because I look just the way I did back in '76.

Out of habit, I reach into my purse for my reading glasses, but they aren't there—I didn't need them back in '76. *Oh, how quickly we forget the beauty of our younger years.*

I dig into the first book, written by a scientist a few years back. He speculates on different theories, which include a machine with the capability of breaking the sound barrier when operated at certain times of the year, when the planets align with certain constellations. He also quotes author H.G. Wells from his novel, **The Time Machine**. I sigh as I read Wells's quote: "Class divisions must be removed before mankind wrecks itself." I take in a deep breath. *If they only knew what was ahead of them.*

I move on to the next book, written by several scientists who mention portals and name places where one might attempt time travel. The Grand Canyon, Sedona, Arizona, and Stonehenge are just a few.

I glance at my watch, noting the time. I need to dash downstairs to check out the microfiche. I remember there was a copy machine in the basement so I carry the books with me to make copies of the pages that held the best information.

The lighting in the basement is poor, just as I remember. There is only one other person here, a young man at the first table.

I grab a spot in the back and search through various articles in some of the science magazines. I don't have much luck until I open up the local YSU paper and find an article on time travel written by a Professor Lowry a few years back, at the same university from which I graduated. I read on with heightened interest and just about fall out of my chair when he mentions a former astronomy teacher from a local high school who was forming a club for those interested in the subject. The name of the club strikes a chord in me, and I remember way back when Dylan had told me he was going to attend one of their meetings with Gregg. Orion's Path was its name, and it was one I couldn't forget.

I shake my head and take notes in the small spiral notebook I brought with me, knowing what I have to do next. I have contacts, but I need to be sure to mention it to Dylan, that is if he ever calls me. Then again, I know he will. It's all a part of this crazy plan.

*No—it's all a part of my destiny.*

I head over to Marcone's to meet Tracey, feeling as if my car knows the places I might want to go and it could drive itself. I head out onto Market Street toward the café. Marcone's was our favorite place to meet. We both loved the fried chicken. *Oh, how I wish I'd eaten healthier back then.* Then again, I used to be so thin it didn't matter. I tell myself to take a deep breath and hope she'll buy my story without referring me to a therapist or a local institution.

Tracey waves me over to a booth she scored in the back by the window. Given my beautiful friend's wide smile on her plump face and long, golden hair cascading way past her shoulders, I don't think I could miss her if I tried. "Wasn't last night a blast?" she asks as she stands to hug me.

"Y. . . yes, it sure was," I respond, trying to hide all of my pent-up emotions.

"I always knew Dylan had a thing for you. I mean, the way he always watches you dance when he plays? I've watched him, and you can't tell me he isn't hot for you."

I'm at a loss for words, so I reply with a simple, "Think so?"

"Damn, girl—you scored! He's going to call you, just wait."

We look at the menu, but I don't know why when we always ordered the same thing: fried chicken, fries, and coleslaw.

The waitress brings us our iced teas, and I decide it's the right time to question my best friend, so I take a deep breath and hope for the best. "Uh…mind if I ask you a personal but odd question?"

"Sure. What's up?" She lifts her glass from the table.

"Did you ever have a strange deja vu experience or feel as if you weren't really in your body?"

"No, not really…what exactly do you mean?" She sets her drink down without taking a sip.

"I mean, like an out-of-body experience. Like you traveled back in time, or to another era."

"You know, Jenn, you had a couple of drinks last night, and you usually only stick to one rum and Coke."

I suck in another deep breath. "No. No! I tell you: something's not right. I'm not supposed to be here!"

"Now, I know you're still feeling the effects of last night. The more I think about it, the more I wonder if someone didn't slip something into your drink."

"Tracey, I'm going to tell you what has happened, and I want you to listen before you say anything. And no, I don't think anyone slipped anything in my drink."

The waitress delivers our plates. I wait until she's out of earshot before I spin my tale, and I don't hold back even a single detail. She listens carefully, but I can tell by the look on her face that none of it is registering.

We take bites in between the breaks of my rant. When I'm finished, she offers me her best answer, and it's not one I want to hear. "You know, you've just spent four years in class, and maybe you need a break before starting to teach. Don't rush things. Take some time off to recoup."

I shrug my shoulders and try to follow her reasoning, but I know I'm getting nowhere, so I tell her what she wants to hear. "Maybe you're right."

"I'm always right," she snaps, spearing a French fry, "and by the way, I'll pick you up at seven sharp. Danger Zone is playing at the Twilight Club tonight."

It seems like the drive home is endless. Traffic is heavy for a Saturday, and I feel the urge to venture over to Mill Creek Park to clear my head. It's where I used to go to study. I wish I'd brought those notes and papers with me.

But logic sets in, and I know I need to head home and go over my notes, as well. The park can wait until tomorrow. That is if I'm still stuck here in this time warp.
Joe's old Volkswagen is in the drive, and I brace myself. It's not going to be easy.

He meets me at the door and gives me one of his huge bear hugs. "How's my favorite sister?"

I pull back and stare into those dark brown eyes, just like Mom's. It's so good to see him again, even if it's a younger version of himself. It's been too long. "I'm your only sister, Joe." I chuckle, and we chat about our weekend plans. He tells me he's leaving soon to attend a Harley meet-up at Lake Erie. I remind him to enjoy himself and stay out of trouble.

Mom and Dad are still out shopping, so I head up to my room, eager to dive back into my notes.

The phone in the hall rings, and I answer. There's no caller ID here, so I don't know it's Dylan before I hear his voice. I freeze when I recognize him.

"Thought you'd forgotten about me," he says in his smooth, velvety voice.

"How could I forget about last night?" I manage to say.

"I'd love for you to accompany me to Midway Park tonight. I know it's last minute, but we were just called to cover for the first band scheduled to play. The lead singer is sick."

My pulse races, and I search for words. "I…I'd love to!"

"Great. Pick you up at six. Oh, and I need your address." Once again, my address flows off of my tongue like silk.

I hang up and lay on my bed, staring at the ceiling. *Uggh, another huge deja vu moment!*

# Chapter 16

Calling Tracey to cancel our evening out is something I dread, but I need a few hours to go back over those notes before my date with Dylan. I decide to call her now to get it out of the way. I always hated having things like that hanging over my head.

"Well, I'm happy for you. And at least you'll be safe. I mean, what happened the other night…I really do think someone slipped something into your drink. That's very scary!"

"Now, I want you to forget about all of this nonsense about something being off and just go and have a good time."

I have to agree with her because there's no way she'll ever understand it. It's even beyond my scope of understanding.

I have a couple of hours to get back to my research before my date. Joe's gone for the weekend, and Mom and Dad have just come home from shopping. I make my way downstairs to inform them I have a date with Dylan. Mom shakes her head but tells me to have a good time. Dad gives me the same old line: "Make sure you tell him I'm an avid hunter."

I laugh and give him a peck on the cheek, knowing darn well he'd never hurt a fly.

I help them unload the groceries and excuse myself to go up to my room to work on resumes. Mom reminds me to be sure to eat something before my date, knowing I'll miss dinner. She's a caring mom, just as I remember her, and an Italian one to boot.

I lay on my bed, perusing my notes, highlighting the things that stand out the most for me: portals, deep meditation, time machines, and sound vibrations.

*Wham!*

*Sound vibrations!*

*Dylan's lyrics at the end of his song, the one I listened to right before I blacked out. That's got to be it! He's the reason I'm here, I'm sure of it.* I remember how the song sounded a bit off and how it was played at a higher pitch that was different from the original version I remember. *Was this the Mandela Effect in action?* More woo woo stuff to fog my brain. It's a good thing I'm seeing Dylan tonight. It's the perfect time to question him about this, and I won't let it go. I can't.

I need to ask him about Orion's Path as well. I don't remember him bringing it up until after we'd been dating for a while, but I'll just ask him if he has ever heard of it.

Time flies. I need to hurry and get dressed.

I rummage through the few dresses I have in my closet, some of which would be considered vintage in my time. I try to decide between a black mini skirt and a white ruffle top or a pair of jeans and a low-cut, long-sleeved silk top.

I pull the black mini skirt and white ruffle top off of their hangers. *Hmm...might be a bit too sexy.* I decide to go with it anyway, as I remember how Dylan always told me he loved it when I dressed sexy.

When I go through my old makeup drawer, some of the items I use in my time are not there. Then again, I'm twenty-four now, and I don't need all that much.

I apply my foundation, blush, and mascara and top it off with frosted pink lip gloss. It was always the frosted pink gloss—we all went for the Mary Quant London look back then.

I blow-dry my hair, trying my best to straighten it, but there's no such thing as a hot iron here. They haven't come out yet, at least, not to my knowledge.

When I'm done, I stand back and check myself out in the hall mirror; not bad, if I do say so myself. Guess I'd post this outfit on social media if such a thing existed.

I grab a sweater and head downstairs to wait for Dylan. Mom and Dad are just finishing dinner, and I sit down with them and have a small plate of pasta, the one dish we always had on weekends. Mom asks me about Dylan, and I tell her she will meet him shortly. My pulse quickens when I hear a loud motor approaching. It must be him and his muscle car. I vaguely remember what make it was, but I do know it was hot and fast. At least, I thought so back then.

Dad remains in the kitchen, reading the paper as the doorbell rings. I let him wait, not wanting to seem over-anxious. When I open the door, I find a rocker decked out in a burgundy silk shirt and tight jeans—damn, he looks fine!

I invite him in and introduce him to Mom. She dries her hands on her flowered apron, shakes his hand, and apologizes for her appearance, informing him she has just finished dinner, just like the mom I remember. She looks great, but it was customary for her to apologize, no matter how she looked.

Mom tells us to have a good time and be safe. I'm rather glad Dad's decided to remain in the kitchen. I remember that my dates never liked being grilled for details.

Dylan opens the car door for me, and I slide into the smooth leather seats in his black Camaro. He puts a hand on my knee, and my insides feel as if they are about to erupt. He starts the ignition, and we are off on our first date…the first of many.

As we pull onto Youngstown-Poland Road, he tells me the details he's planned for the night. "You'll be able to stay in the hosting room if you like—it'll be warmer in there—or you can hang out down by the stage."

I turn in my seat to face him. "You know I'm going to be right down there in front. I wouldn't miss hearing you sing."

He turns to me and flashes his deep hazel eyes. "We'll leave after the second set, when the second band takes over. I've made reservations at Fortuna's."

Fortuna's was my favorite restaurant on the 422 Strip back in the day. Nobody could cook Italian food better than Mom, but that place ran a close second. *Even though I already had some pasta at home I figure I'll simply order something light.* I read that it had been torn down not too long ago, and I wonder if getting to revisit these places in their heyday isn't some sort of blessing in disguise.

He asks me if everything is okay, and I tell him I'm fine—I'll save launching the Spanish Inquisition until after dinner.

# Chapter 17

I'm glad I brought a sweater. I've opted to stand outside, and there's a chill in the air. *How could I not be out there to listen to the band?* I find a seat on one of the wooden benches outside of a small café right inside the amusement park. It's odd being here with all of the rides shut down. The park closes at five but remains open for events after that. I feel a prickly sensation run up my spine. This place holds so many memories from my childhood being we always came here to celebrate special occasions.

The park isn't as packed as usual, so I can enjoy the performance without being squished like a sardine. When the band plays their second song, I feel that old urge coming on, the one that brought out the wild side in me, and I know exactly why. It's the music, especially Dylan's music. I move up to the platform and begin to sway, letting my body follow the rhythm.

I look up and hold Dylan's gaze with mine. He winks at me, and I am more energized than ever. I realize I have a few spectators, which is nothing new. A middle-aged man with a long beard manages to work his way up toward me and starts dancing with me. I don't want to be rude, so I keep on dancing, knowing that Dylan's eyes are on me even while he's playing.

The bearded man edges in closer, and I try not to look at him and move farther away, hoping he'll get the message.

When the song is over, I walk back toward the bench to take a breather, and the man follows me. He stumbles as he walks, and I smell alcohol on his breath as he speaks. "I like your moves," he mumbles.

Ryan, one of the band's roadies, heads my way to ask if the man is bothering me. I tell him he hasn't done anything wrong, but I'd like for him to leave me alone.

The man looks at me and then at Ryan. "Didn't know Ablaze had so many fucking damn rules!" he shouts, throwing his hands in the air.

I pray there's not a scene, but then the man shakes his head and walks off. I watch as he heads for the entrance.

I thank Ryan for coming to my rescue and decide to sit out the next song, which is their last one of the evening. I'm eager to leave, get to the restaurant, and question Dylan.

"Dark Wicked Woman" is the last song, as it usually is. My ears perk up, and my heart races as I listen to the words. Once more, I'm struck by how different the lyrics are from the CD Dylan sent to my home.

I get goosebumps on my arms. *It's all making sense now.*

*How crazy is it that he had the whole thing planned out? He knew exactly what he was doing. He brought me here! But how? Why?*

Once again, my mind wanders back to the night before I was transported. It was *that song,* I know it! Especially that little sing-songy chant at the end. His voice sounded so different on the recording, not to mention that there had to have been something in the words. I have to find out. *Is he involved with some type of cult or using dark magic?*

My nerves are set on edge at the mere thought of it.

While Dylan changes, I wait for him outside the pavilion. It's already 8 p.m. We have reservations for 8:30.

Dylan emerges in a pair of jeans and a dark green, long-sleeved knit jersey. He puts a hand on my shoulder, and we walk out to the parking lot. He mentions the strange man who bothered me earlier. I ask if he's jealous, and he responds with that crooked smile. "Ya got a hot body, babe," he says, "can't say as I blame him. And yes, it bothered me. I wanted to kick the shit outta him."

I'm quiet on the way to the restaurant. Dylan notices and asks me if anything is wrong. I tell him I'm just thinking about how good the band sounded tonight.

*God, I'm good at lying.*

* * *

We pull into Fortuna's parking lot, which is unusually empty. It's a good thing because when I start to question Dylan, things might get a bit crazy, and I don't need an audience. The hostess leads us to a table in the back. We pass by several large Roman statues and an ornate white fountain in the center of the room on the way. The air is filled with the aroma of garlic and fresh-baked bread. The table has a romantic feel, with the checkered red tablecloth and a candle set in a crystal vase in the center.

The waiter fills our glasses with water and hands us our menus. He sounds off the specials for the night, but I'm too focused on my mission tonight to hear a word he says.

Dylan taps my hand, jolting me out of my trance. I order a glass of white wine, and he orders a Bordeaux.

His hazel eyes seem to sparkle in the candlelight. *This guy is so hot.* I've forgotten what he used to do—and still does—to my body. I'm actually getting turned on right here! I try to focus and remain on track, but it's the chemistry we had and still have.

I wait until I've had a few sips of my wine before posing my first question, tucking a few loose strands of hair behind my ear and taking a deep breath. "Dylan…I…uh…want to ask you something very serious."

He gives me an incredulous look. "Sure, what's wrong?"

"Does anything about our meeting at the Regal Room and this date seem off to you?"

He waits before responding. "Off in what way? What do you mean?"

"I mean, does it seem like this is some sort of dream to you?"

He grabs my hand. "Babe, this *is* a dream. You're the dream. I mean, what man wouldn't be proud to be with you? Just look at you—you're a knockout!"

I sigh.

The waiter comes to get our orders, and I wait until he's out of earshot before I continue. "Thank you, but this is serious! What if I told you I came here from the future?"

"Okay, what were you drinking at the concert…or smoking?"

"Nothing. I swear! I don't know if you'll understand any of this, but I'm going to tell you everything that happened before I landed in the Regal Room the other night, right there in the ladies' room."

"*If you're from the future, can you predict things such as wars, floods, and plagues?" I hope my jesting encourages her to stop. I can't have her in this mindset—gotta stop her searching for answers here.*

My body goes cold when he utters the word 'plague', and I tell him every detail while he sips his wine. My mention of the pandemic doesn't seem to faze him too much.  He seems more attentive when I tell him about the CD he'd sent me, with him singing those odd lyrics and the weird tone of his voice. I pray what I say sinks in and he'll have some answers for me.

He sets his glass down and tilts his head to the side, shaking his long bangs out of his eyes. "I know you may be into some New Age mystical stuff, and I can dig it. I can tell you I'm into astrology and have been invited to a new group meeting called Orion's Path. It's more science than science fiction, and I'm seriously thinking of going. I think you are trying way too hard to read something bizarre into this rather than accept the fact that we have some strong chemistry between us. That's all."

I shake my head. *This is futile. Why even try?* If he has done something to me, he'll never tell, but he did mention Orion's Path.

Our food comes, but I've lost most of my appetite. Dylan scoots his chair closer to me, spears a ravioli, and brings it to my lips. "Come on, babe—they make the best ravioli here. Take a bite."

I accept his offer, and it does taste good. The flavors virtually explode in my mouth, and I decide to calm down and finish my meal. Maybe I'll get more answers as the date wears on.

After paying the bill, Dylan informs me that his roommate has gone for the weekend and suggests we stop at his apartment for a nightcap. I want to get home and go back over my notes, but it's hard to say no to him. Besides, I figure I might find some leads once we're at his apartment. The last time I was there was too long ago, and I don't even remember what the place looked like. It would be good to get another glimpse of it.

We pull into the midsized brick complex, and he parks in a numbered spot—his, I assume. He opens the door, and we walk to his upstairs apartment. I'm thankful it's only on the second floor. These platform shoes are killing me—*how did I ever wear these things, let alone dance in them?*

Dylan flicks on the light. He takes my hand, leads me to the large, overstuffed plaid sofa, and offers me a drink, but I decline. I've already had too much wine. I'm a bit lightheaded and need to sit down.

I close my eyes, take a deep breath, and Dylan's lips meet mine. Our lips part, and his tongue dances with mine. It's like some kind of hot tango.

He leans me into the far end of the sofa and plants little kisses along my neck. I throw my head back, enjoying the electrifying sensation. It seems as though the hormones I had back in my twenties have kicked in. His hand slips into my jeans and finds a resting spot inside my lace panties. His fingers enter me, and he plays with my clit as though it was his finely-tuned guitar. It feels so damn good that I moan with delight.

I want to make him feel good, as well, so I pull down his jeans. His member is rock hard. *God, it's beautiful.*

I take it into my hands and work it using a combination of soft and hard strokes.

When we are both on the brink of coming, he pulls out a condom from his pocket and slips it on. We are on the high-pile shag rug when he enters me slowly, but once he's in, he rides me hard and fast. I call out his name, which only strengthens his fervor. He pulls out, enters me again, and asks if I'm ready. "Hell, yes!" I yell.

It's been one hell of a night. After I use his bathroom to clean up, I tell him I need to get home. All I want is to shower and go to bed...my bed.

He tells me he needs to see me again. Tells me I'm his addiction.

I kiss him goodnight in the driveway, and he waits until I'm inside the house before pulling away.

I walk quietly up the stairs, knowing Mom and Dad are in bed—it's way past 2 a.m.

I use the shower downstairs so as not to wake them. I'm not in the mood to answer any questions, besides.

When I'm done, I wrap the thick, fluffy towel around myself and head upstairs to my room. It's chilly, so I slip into a long, flannel gown I find in my dresser and plop into bed. I'm too tired to even try to decipher why I'm still here. *Maybe tomorrow will be a more insightful day.*

With that thought, I'm out like a light.

# Chapter 18

I wake to voices coming from Mom and Dad's room and glance at the clock to see it's 9 a.m. They always went to early mass on Sundays. I used to go, but as I got older, Mom said it was my choice. Though I might have lost interest, I never lost my faith.

Mom tells Dad to wear his navy-blue blazer. She always took care of him. It was her thing, or possibly another one of those Italian things. I was maybe fifty percent the same—I babied Mark, which certainly didn't help our marriage, particularly after he decided that cheating was permissible.

I decide to stay in bed and pretend to be asleep, knowing they won't wake me. I'll listen for the door to close, get myself a cup of coffee, and go back over the notes. With Joe still gone, I know I'll have peace and quiet which will allow me to focus.

As soon as I hear the garage door close, I look through my bedroom window to see the white Oldsmobile backing out of the driveway, throw on my robe, and head downstairs. There's still coffee in the pot, so I pour myself a cup, grab a slice of Mom's homemade sweetbread, and head back upstairs. I've forgotten how good this bread tastes. The sweetness and buttery texture leaves my mouth watering for another piece, but I decide to wait until lunch. We didn't worry too much about carbs back in the day.

My thoughts go back to Dylan last night when I questioned him. He was a bit evasive and dismissed my concerns. *Does he really not know, or is he playing a role so I won't find him out? He's a darn good actor if this is the case.*

I've been here three days already. Since then, I've recorded my notes in the notebook I found right alongside with my old journal I kept in my nightstand. I take some time to read those old passages and all it does is make me more emotional. Letting this feeling pass I know I've got work to do.

I dive back into the notes and copied papers and read more about out-of-body experiences and remote viewing. This one article states that our military used remote viewing during WWII—*how interesting is that?* I watched some YouTube videos about it—where was YouTube when you needed it?

My only hope is to go to the university tomorrow and try to speak to Professor Lowry, the man who wrote the article in the paper on the microfiche. Hopefully, he'll have some answers for me.

I go back to my notes and focus on the astrology aspect of time travel and how the stars must align with the portals. *Had the stars been in alignment the night I got dizzy in my living room? Was the restroom at the Regal Room a portal?* It was all too confusing. I miss Brandy and my life back home, but I'm home here, as well. If I were stuck here in my past life without a way to get back home, would it all play out as it did back then? *Would I get married to Mark and give birth to Brandy in this time period?*

That won't be for three years yet.

The upside of all this is that I'm getting time to spend with my parents…my deceased parents!

The sound of the garage door startles me, and I shove the papers under my bed and try to pull myself together and get dressed before facing Mom and Dad again.

They greet me with big smiles and hugs. It's no surprise that Mom asks me if I had anything to eat.

We all sit down at the kitchen table, and she makes a fresh pot of coffee as Dad re-reads the Sunday paper. Mom asks me about my date last night, and I tell her everything except the details of my sexual encounter.

"I'm happy for you, Jenn," she says. "You know, Dylan seems like a nice young man. I hope he's thinking of another profession in the future. A musician won't fetch a good income to provide for a family. He won't make enough if he's thinking ahead."

I knew that was coming. I'd heard it before, and several times at that. "It's nothing serious, Mom. It's only been one date. Who knows where it will lead?" I set my mug down on the plastic rooster-printed tablecloth. There are roosters in every nook, cranny, and corner of the kitchen. Mom loved them. I remember when Joe and I had the estate sale after her death, and Joe asked me if I wanted them. I was not into collectibles or any type of knick-knacks, but how I wish I'd kept at least one. Joe wound up taking most of them, and I was glad he did.

"So, what are your plans for today?" Mom asks as she cuts herself a slice of sweet bread.

I pause to construct a plausible story. "I think I'm going to call Tracey to see if she'd like to meet me at Mill Creek Park."

"That's a wonderful idea, hon. I think it'll do you good. To be honest, I've been a bit worried about you. You haven't been yourself these past few days."

*If only she knew.*

I retreat to my room and give Tracey a call. She agrees to meet me at one in Lanterman's Mill's side parking lot. "I hope you're not going to talk crazy like you did the other night," her voice booms.

"Crazy talk? Nah. Just want to hang with my good friend," I lie…again.

It's going to be a warm day for the end of September, and the park is just the place I need for some grounding. I decide to leave a bit early, hoping it will give me some time to think things through before she arrives.

* * *

I'd forgotten just how beautiful this place is. The tall pines and oaks stand so majestically, and the mill's still running. It was built in 1799 for grinding corn and wheat. It continues to be a famous icon for beautiful parks in Ohio.

I stand in the parking lot in awe of the history of it all. When I'm ready, I walk a bit, my small backpack slung over my shoulder, to scope out a good spot to spread out my blanket and spend more time taking in the sights and sounds and thinking about history and how I'm living it…again.

As I sit and glance back at the mill, it dawns on me: What if this place is one of those portals I read about? It's not mentioned in the notes, but they claim there are several of them all over the planet. I know water is an energy magnet—*maybe this will be the portal that will transport me back?*

Off in the distance, I spot Tracey walking toward the pathway from the mill, her long, golden blonde hair bouncing with every step. She has that same large black shoulder bag with her. In it, she always carried an extra reserve of makeup. I used to tease her that she even had the kitchen sink in there.

I force myself to act as normal as possible but plan to slip in some casual questions during our visit.

We talk about my date last night, and she's most eager to hear the details. Being my best friend, I tell her about the sex. I have to—not for her sake, but it does me good to tell someone. It's something true that I can explain.

I pull out two small thermoses of iced tea and a bag of Italian cookies. Tracey loves those, too, but she wants to hear more details about the date before she takes a bite.

"I hope you slept well. I thought you needed some rest," she says.

I sigh. "You know, I'm not sure exactly what I need. When I told you something was off the other night, I meant it. It seems as if I'm in some sort of dream, and I can't wake up."

She shakes her head. "If this is a dream, then it's one hell of a long one. At least, for you."

"I don't think it's a dream. When I told you what happened to me the night I played the CD and ended up in the restroom at the Regal Room, it was all true."

She grabs my arm. "Listen, Jenn—maybe you do need to see a therapist or even your regular doctor. Tell your mom. I know she'll make you an appointment, I'll even go with you."

I pull back, knowing I'm spinning my wheels here, and I don't want it to escalate into an argument, so we go back to talking about Dylan. She's all ears when I tell her that he wants to have another date, but I don't know what he has planned.

We're sitting for a good two hours before Tracey announces she has to go home to get ready for work tomorrow—the small boutique she's been working at has extended her hours. I tell her I'll call her the minute I hear from Dylan, and we plan a tentative girl's night out for next Friday.

I wait until she's gone before gathering up my things to walk by the old mill. The rushing water in the creek soothes me. I want to check out the museum and the small gift shop again—I remember the gift shop was my favorite part when my class went on a field trip in grade school.

Stuffed, mounted birds and other mammals still grace the walls and rafters of this dusty museum, but it's less scary now since I was last here. As a child, I was always afraid of this place, but it somehow doesn't have the same effect now.

Noting my time, I leave the museum and head out to the parking lot, walking toward the Roadrunner. It's not long before I have the urge to turn around to look at the mill one more time. At that exact moment, a sudden wind kicks up, blowing my hair about—*could this place possibly be my way back?*

# Chapter 19

Sunday evenings always meant Mom's homemade spaghetti and meatballs. The garlicky sauce smells heavenly when I walk in the door. I make my way over to the stove, where Mom is plopping in the meatballs in a large pot. "Did you have a good time with Tracey?"

I tell her about our relaxing visit but leave out the part about the possibility of the mill being a portal. *Would she even believe me?* Regardless, I'm not going there. I'm just happy to spend time with my family again. If I'm going to be stuck here, then I figure it's due to a time glitch, and maybe this was all meant to happen.

Dad is outside chatting with the neighbor, and I know Joe won't get home until early tomorrow morning. I tell Mom I'm heading up to my room to finalize my resume for substitute teaching to take to the district office tomorrow. I already have solid excuses lined up. In a way, I feel bad I have to resort to lies, but it's a part of survival, I reason.

I need answers.

I make more notes in my notebook about attempting to see Professor Lowry at YSU tomorrow. It's a long shot that I'll get to see him, but if I could just make an appointment with him, I would consider it a win. I read back over the papers about portals, noting how astrology plays a huge part in all of this. Thinking back to what Dylan said the other night has me wondering—*had he said he was interested in astrology and going to join a club? Could he be playing me for a fool? Did he use some sort of magic to get me here? Whether he did or not, why do I want to see him again? Was he right about the chemistry between us?* The sex was incredible—*maybe he used some kind of sex magic on me?* I've read about that, and it's truly a dark art.

After all these years, I'd forgotten what it felt like having sex with him but experiencing it here and now is incredible! It's like we have this unforgettable chemistry.

I feel lightheaded again and decide to take a quick nap before supper.

Dad sits at the dinner table in a white T-shirt and plaid pajama bottoms, his usual at-home uniform. He tells me how proud he is that I'm already seeking a job so soon after graduation.

After helping Mom with the dishes, I tell her I'm planning on leaving early in the morning to go to the district office, so I'll miss them at breakfast.

I toss and turn most of the night—too much on my mind, I guess. I open my window, and a gentle breeze ushers in some calm, allowing me to sleep.

I'm excited yet nervous about what I've got planned for today. I pull out a dressy pair of black pants and a white tailored shirt—gotta look the part. Maybe I'll get lucky at the university with a more polished appearance. As I'm brushing my hair, I think about how all of this is going to play out—I am reliving my past, after all. I'll have to take my resume to the district office and apply—that's how my teaching career all got started. I've read articles about people who supposedly time-traveled to try to change the past, but that's ill-advised as the experts claim it could result in major catastrophes.

In the end, I decide that I will, indeed, drop by to hand in my resume. It is the last week of September, after all, and I'm sure they will need substitutes very soon.

Pulling into the parking deck of the university is a no-brainer—I still have my YSU parking sticker on my windshield. I get out of the car, head toward the main science building, and speak to the lady behind the desk with the large-framed glasses dangling from a sparkly chain. "May I help you?"

I tell her I'd like to find Professor Lowry.

She asks me if I have an appointment, and I tell her no.

She motions for me to have a seat and punches some numbers into the phone, trying, I assume, to reach his secretary. My eyes refuse to leave her, and I remind myself to breathe and hope my plan will go somewhere.

She clicks off the phone and tells me the professor has a full schedule today and won't be able to meet with me until the following week.

I sigh and ask, "What's the earliest day possible?"

She tells me it won't be until the following Monday.

She phones the professor's office again, puts his secretary on hold, and asks me about the nature of my visit.

"Tell them I'm most interested in an article he wrote for the university paper on time travel. I'm doing some research myself."

She gives me a nod and informs the secretary of my purpose for the visit.

She confirms that I have an appointment next Monday, and I thank her and head out for the parking deck. Since I have time to spare, I plan to head over to the district office to hand in my resume.

My heart races as I close the Road Runner's door, and I sit there, frozen in my seat. Flashbacks come quickly to the forefront.

I was in this parking deck when I backed out and hit the car behind me. But I don't remember when that exactly happened. *Damn this time glitch!*

*Do I look behind me and wait? I don't want to go through that again.* Our insurance went up after that fender bender. To be on the safe side I take precautions and look behind me. No backup cameras in this car.

I back out carefully, avoiding any mishaps.

* * *

I check my makeup in the mirror and add a fresh coat of lipstick, the frosted pink one I have in my shoulder bag. I wish this color was still on the market in my time. I pull on a sweater and head for the main entrance to the district office. I remember them telling me they needed subs right away when I phoned them.

A stout older woman with huge, wire-rimmed glasses greets me, has me sign in and take a seat, and asks if I have an appointment. She tells me it will be around a twenty-minute wait.

As I wait, I tap my foot on the tile floor and think about how the whole educational system has changed since the seventies. My later years of teaching had me dealing with quite a few challenging students, as well as parents.

A tall, thin, middle-aged man comes over to greet me and asks me to follow him to his office. I enter a smaller office with a large window that faces the parking lot, and he ushers me to the seat across from his desk.

I hand him my resume, and he studies it, raising his head to ask me a few questions about my experience. He informs me that I will need to take a two-day training course from the district before I can begin subbing. I tell him that's fine, and he hands me a schedule of the dates and times for the substitute training.

He asks me if I have any questions, which I don't, being that I already know the drill. He thanks me for my interest in the district and says he looks forward to having me on board. He shakes my hand, and I thank him.

I head out to the car; glad I have tangible proof I was here. At least I didn't lie…this time. But who knows how long I'll be here—I could possibly be gone tomorrow. I have all week to look forward to meeting with the professor. I'm banking on him having answers, or it's back to the library for more research.

I pull into the driveway and see Joe's Harley parked in the garage. He and his buddy are sitting at the picnic table where we always hung out. He stands up and hugs me. "And how's my favorite sister?"

"I'm fine. You crack me up." I laugh and hug him back.

He asks me if all went well with the sub interview. I show him the paperwork, and he gives me a high-five before I excuse myself to go get undressed. I kiss Mom on the cheek as I walk by her while she's on the phone. She's still dressed from work. Her job as a receptionist at a dental office gave me some pretty good perks, like no waiting whenever I needed an appointment. Dad wouldn't be home from his job as a mail carrier until five.

It's another warm day for late September, so I change into some cut-off jean shorts and a T-shirt, having a good chuckle when I look at the size label: a size four. I guess I forgot how thin I was. That's one thing I wish had stayed with me into my later years.

The hall phone rings, and I pick it up, surprised to hear Dylan's voice.

"Hey, babe!" he says. "I've missed you."

I go silent. It's only been two days—*is he serious?*

He asks what I've been up to, and I tell him about my day. He tells me he needs a favor, and if I say no, it's okay, but he'd like me to think about it.

I know what's coming—how could I ever forget? It's been one of my fondest yet craziest memories, one I've repeatedly told my closest friends, excluding Brandy and Mark.

"We have a gig at the Stardust Room Saturday night, and well, you know what it's like. You've been there."

I say yes and listen to his voice.

"I'd love to show you off by having you be one of the go-go girls. I mean, you are a great dancer."

I don't know what to say. "I'm honored, but I don't know if I can do it."

"What do you mean? You just get a costume and let loose."

*Let loose?* I think about that for a minute. I took jazz lessons all through high school, but cage dancing is on a totally different level.

He waits for my answer. I tell him I don't even own a costume like that. The only thing I do have that comes even close are my old white ankle boots.

"You'll think of something. You have an entire week. Just think about being up there in that cage and dancing to our music. All eyes will be on you." He sounds so convincing, and he's damn good at it.

"I...I dunno. Let me think about this one. I'll call you back tomorrow."

He tells me we can go to dinner after the show, my pick, of course."

After we hang up, I sit on my bed thinking about the conversation. I won't say no because I accepted his offer in the past and had the best time of my life. It was the only time I was ever in a cage, dancing at a seventies club. How many people can say they've done that?

Mom stands in the hallway, asking me if I have another date with Dylan.

I tell her it's a dinner date and that's all. She's happy for me but doesn't press on with another lecture of dating a musician. If she only knew her daughter planned to be a go-go girl on Saturday night, she'd probably lose it.

# Chapter 20

It's good to sit and chat with Joe at dinner. He talks about his weekend at the bike meet and how he enjoys being a motorcycle mechanic for his buddies. I shake my head when I hear about all the fights, drinking, and loose women. When I ask him what his plans are now that he has graduated from high school, he tells me he plans to attend a trade school. I inquire about the nature of his study, and he tells me it's in auto mechanics—why am I not surprised? He loves what he does, and it will have a major payoff in the future, but I cannot tell him that.

Mom breaks into the conversation to serve her famous meatloaf. It always was one of my favorites. It's the sauce. It's always been her sauce.

I cut a hefty slice and scoop up some roasted potatoes and carrots.

Joe shifts the conversation to Dylan. "I hear you're dating a local rock star."

"Well, not sure if he's a star yet, but we've only had one date and possibly another one coming up."

"Should we start planning the wedding?" he jokes.

I throw my napkin at him and tell him to knock it off.

Dad interrupts. "Just as long as he stays in line."

"Yeah. Just let us know if we need to straighten him out," Joe adds.

"I'm fine. *We're* fine. I can take care of myself," I say, getting up to pour myself a refill of iced tea.

After dinner, I go up to my room and call Tracey. I'm anxious to tell her about my upcoming date with Dylan, but I hesitate before calling. I glance around my bedroom with its pink and green accents and sigh. *This was my safe place for so many years. It still smells like my old standby perfume. I wonder if it's still available? Maybe on eBay.* I'll have to check it out if I ever get back home.

Tracey's voice is a welcome one. I tell her about my upcoming date, and she has loads of questions, as always. With my door closed, I feel confident in divulging the details.

"You lucky dog, you! That's the experience of a lifetime!" she shouts.

I chuckle inwardly. *Yes, it will be, especially when the club gets raided.* That part, I'll never forget, but I leave that detail out. She'll be there, of course, and I wouldn't want to cause her any worries. If she knew, she wouldn't show up.

She tells me she has a brilliant idea for my costume, and I listen, knowing exactly what it entails. "You've got that new blue paisley bikini, so we'll get some fringes at the fabric shop, and you can sew them to the top and bottom. Problem solved."

I tell her she's a sheer genius and a great best friend. I also tell her she will be my guest that night. I promise to call Dylan to let him know. We make plans to go to Miller's Fabrics tomorrow. I hang up and pull out my blue bikini from the dresser.

I remember it well. It was one of my favorites, with its blue paisley design. I hold it up against my body, glancing in the dresser mirror. It suits me well.

I shake my body, imagining how the suit will move once I sew on the fringes.

I glance over to my record player over in the corner. I realize I need to practice some moves, so I pull out a Deep Purple album and start to bust a few moves, keeping the volume low and the door locked. I don't need anyone coming in as I get into my zone.

It's funny how moving to the music comes easily for me. It always did. I'm pretty sure I know all of the numbers Dylan's band will play, and it'll be easy to improvise if there are any new songs. It feels as if I've been dancing to these same songs forever now.

With all the excitement, I've forgotten about my research, so I spread my papers over the bed and dive back into my notebook, intent on spending some time going back over the notes on portals.

Lanterman's Mill comes back to mind. I need to head back over there again myself. If the place is a portal, I'll need to know how to access it. I'll drive over there tomorrow after Tracey and I get our things from the fabric store.

I notice it's getting late. I've been up in my room for two hours now, so I decide to head downstairs, make some tea, and sit with Mom and Dad before bed. I want to relish every moment I have left with them. Who knows when I'll pop back into my time zone, if ever? And I think about what is real. Both places are indeed real, and I'm stuck between these two realms.

Mom makes a fresh pot of coffee and brews a cup of tea for me. I hug her tightly and feel a rush of tears filling my eyes. I don't want to let her go.

"What's wrong, dear?" she asks, sounding concerned.

I hold her gaze. "It seems like time is going by so fast. It won't be long before I have a job, and I'll be out in an apartment and on my own." It's the best response I can come up with.

We take our cups into the living room as Dad sits at the table with his newspaper. There's a cool breeze coming in through the front screen door. She asks me if I have any place in mind for an apartment and tells me she'd like for me to stay at home until I've saved up enough money from teaching.

They've always been great parents. They paid my entire way through college, and I've never wanted for anything. I move closer to her on the sofa and run my hand through her shiny silver hair.

My emotions are on full alert again. *Do I really want to find a way back? What if I have no choice?* My stomach is doing flip-flops as she grabs my hand and tells me how much she loves me. It's her touch that brings some semblance to my thoughts—at least for now.

# Chapter 21

Tracey and I peruse all the trimmings at Miller's Fabrics. We look at tassels and other bling stacked on the shelves. Tracey points to a rack of white fringe trimming in the next aisle. "This is just the ticket!" You'd think she was the one cage dancing this weekend.

I hold up a piece of the trimmings, examining it closely, and know she's right. We signal a saleslady to cut me four yards. I figure it's better to have some leftovers than not enough.

Feeling as if we've accomplished our task, we decide to head over to have lunch at Marcone's. The smell of fried chicken takes reign over my senses and my stomach. We sit in a booth by the window. The place isn't crowded, so I know we can have a private chat. I can't hold back what I need to say, even knowing I'll get the same response from my friend as the last time.

"It's… it's the same thing I asked you about last time. I know this all sounds weird, but I know I don't belong here."

"What the hell does that mean? You are here, and so am I."

I realize that was a poor way to start. "Okay, let me rephrase that. I mean that I was here in the past, but *this* is the past for me. I have somehow been transported back here from the year 2023."

She looks at me as if I'm crazy.

The waitress comes with water and asks us what we'd like. We order our usual Cokes and the fried chicken lunch special.

As soon as the waitress is out of earshot, Tracey grabs my hand from across the table. "Look, Jenn, last time I said that someone might have put something in your drink, but I'd have thought it would have worn off by now. This is getting out of hand. I'm really worried about you. Have you spoken to your folks about this?"

"No. I can't. It's too complicated. I'd get too emotional."

"Well, you need to pull yourself together. You're going to start teaching soon, and you can't do that with this mindset. Maybe you need to see a therapist."

I search for words without much luck. "Maybe I will." I figure the conversation is going nowhere, so I might as well go along with her.

After I drop Tracey off, I head to Mill Creek Park to check out Lanterman's Mill one more time, now that I've read a bit more about portals.

The park is pretty much deserted for a Tuesday. The weather has warmed up since morning, but the sky is still cloudy. I park and walk over to the mill. My research said the best time to open portals is at night when aligned with a certain constellation, but I don't know if I'd feel safe coming down here at night alone.

Why didn't I take that astronomy class?

I stand and watch the old wooden wheel make its creaky churns and listen to the sound of the water rustling. There's a calm here that overtakes me as if I have some connection to it. I sit on the grass and close my eyes, imagining the night I left home and ended up in The Regal Room in a restroom stall. I envision myself dancing to Dylan's song. It's almost as if I hear his words echo in the water, and I feel drowsy and have to lie down.

A man's voice says, "Miss? Miss, are you okay?" and I open my eyes to see an older man with white hair hovering over me in a green uniform.

"Y-yes. I just got sleepy." I sit up, rub my eyes, and my vision clears.

"Good to hear. I'm the mill attendant here." He stares at me as if trying to gauge my condition. "You sure? I mean, I can call someone."

"No, no, not needed. I'm fine." I stand to let him know all is okay.

He tells me he'll walk me to my car just to make sure I'm okay to drive, and I accept his offer.

At my car, I thank him, climb in, take a deep breath, start the engine, and drive off. All seems to be fine.

My mind clears even more once I pull onto the highway, and my thoughts drift back to the old caretaker. I'm sure he knows the history of the place. I decide to return another time to ask him some questions later on when I don't look like a crazy person.

It's almost five when I arrive home. I leave my bag in the car so I won't have to explain what I bought. Not gonna go there.

Mom is prepping for dinner. Dad hasn't come home from work yet. I ask her if she needs help, but she's got it all under control. She tells me Joe is out for the evening.

I head upstairs to change for dinner, excited to spend that evening sewing the fringes on my bikini.

Having that big lunch with Tracey hasn't left me with much of an appetite, but I can't turn down sitting with Mom and Dad. I pick at the tuna casserole I was always so crazy about.

After dinner, I grab Mom's sewing box, scramble up the stairs to my room, and shut the door. I sit on the floor next to my bed and pull out my blue paisley bikini and the bag from Millers. If anyone comes in the door, I'll slip the bikini under the bed. I don't feel good about keeping secrets from the two people I love the most, but where would I even start? And why would I want to ruin what I have here, be it temporary or permanent?

After meticulously stitching the final row of fringes onto the bikini's bottom piece, I slip into my freshly crafted costume and stand before my dresser mirror. A thrill courses through me as I execute a playful shimmy, causing my fringes to sway in a lively dance of their own. I sweep my hair up into a pile atop my head and practice a series of alluring moves.

The anticipation bubbles up within me, echoing the beat of the music as I stride over to my record player and set the needle carefully down on the Deep Purple album, the volume down low. The familiar notes trickle into the room, and I feel an electric connection between the music and my movements. It's as if my body already knows the choreography, and I effortlessly surrender to the rhythm, losing myself in the dance.

A thought crosses my mind: I didn't conceive this dazzling routine. Every sway, every twirl, is organic, as if this is exactly where I'm supposed to be. The forthcoming Saturday night looms—it's an event that promises to be unforgettable—yet in all this excitement, I'm aware of the dark history hanging over the club. Most know of its tawdry reputation and the fact that it was owned by one of the biggest mobsters in the Youngstown area.

Recollections of a time with flashing lights and the heavy footsteps of law enforcement mar my euphoric surge. I remember the tension, chaos, and abrupt disruption of that night. While my heart races with anticipation for the performance ahead, the sobering undercurrent of caution tugs at my thoughts. It's a reminder that euphoria is fleeting.

Saturday night approaches, as does the opportunity to relive history. The fusion of excitement and awareness churns within me as I prepare to once more dance under the vibrant lights, reclaiming the stage, determined to make this time different, to make it truly unforgettable.

# Chapter 22

I feel an anxiety attack approaching as I pull into the guest parking at YSU. My stomach rumbles, and it's not from hunger. The thought of meeting with Professor Lowry has my nerves going at full speed.

I grab my notebook and head for the science center, pulling my fringed knit poncho tightly around me. It's a chilly morning for the first week of October. I've missed the seasons.

I head down the walkway lined with the large, tall oaks that had subtly started to take on new colors.

While rehearsing my introduction in my head, I'm halted by a student calling out my name from across the lawn. The sun impedes my view of who that person might be, and I have to squint against the sun. "Jennifer? Jennifer!" the voice shouts.

The young man comes closer into view, and I don't recognize him. "What are you doing here?" he asks.

I'm speechless. It's been years since I was in college here—*how could I remember this tall young man with strong Latin features?*

"Congratulations on your graduation. Are you here to enroll in some post-grad work?" he asks, sliding his Ray Bans up over his eyes to rest atop his head.

"I…uh…no. Here to get some transcripts," I lie…again.

"In the science hall? I thought you were an education major." His dark eyes bore into mine.

*How in the hell does he know that?* I wonder if he's been stalking me.

"Yes, but I was considering taking an astrology class. I have read some books, and I have taken an interest in them."

"Awesome! If you want to sign up for a good class, be sure to get into Professor Lowry's class—he's the bomb!"

"So, I've heard."

Another student calls out to the stranger, "Hey, Paul—wait up."

It's a lucky break, as I have no idea who this guy is, other than his name is Paul. He is good-looking, I have to admit. I can't help but notice the strong jawline and the dimple in his chin that forms when he speaks.

I tell Paul it was nice seeing him, but I need to head off. I don't wait to see what the other young man wants with him. He tells me he hopes to run into me sometime again and thanks me for the notes I shared with him in literature class.

I shake my head, trying to remember him, but my mind is blank. I met so many people when I was last here, but that's not important now. I have a meeting to get to, and I need to remain calm and collected or the professor will most likely blow me off as some crazed fan of his.

The front desk secretary takes my name, and I have a seat on the wooden bench again. I tap my foot, trying to control my nerves. My hands are sweaty, and as I grab the notebook, it falls on the floor. Before I have the chance to retrieve it, Paul is handing it back to me.

I thank him and he takes a seat next to me. "I wanted to speak to you before you ran off."

It's not the perfect timing, Paul, I want to say. I can't let anything distract me from getting back to my time, but he's oblivious to this.

He tells me how impressed he was with my writing I had shared in class. *If he only knew that I would be an accomplished writer in the future.*

I thank him and try to avoid any more eye contact or conversation with him.

The secretary calls my name, telling me Professor Lowry is ready to see me now.

Paul looks at me quizzically when I tell him goodbye and walk through the door, following the secretary down a long hallway I assume will lead to the professor's office.

When I get to Lowry's office, an elderly balding man is sitting behind a large metal desk. He tells me to have a seat across from him.

His secretary informs him that he has only thirty minutes until his meeting, and she closes the door, leaving me here with the professor…alone.

"And what brings you here, Miss Kovich?" he asks.

Hearing what his secretary had just said, I know I'm on borrowed time, so I tell him I've read his article in the newspaper archives and was very impressed.

He asks me if I'm interested in taking a class.

I take a deep breath and tell him I'm here for a different reason, that I'm most interested in time portals.

I must have piqued his interest as he stands and walks out from behind his desk and over to the large window overlooking the west end of the campus. He adjusts his wire-rimmed glasses and sits on the edge of his desk, facing me. "I've taken the liberty to view your school records before our meeting. My secretary has pulled them up for me. I see you have recently graduated with a major in elementary education."

"Yes, I have," I utter my response softly.

"So, tell me: what, exactly, do you have in mind for your interest in time portals?"

I take a deep breath and feel my shoulders rise and fall. He watches me, waiting for a response. "Okay…here goes," I say. I know time is of the essence, and I reason that I have nothing to lose. I've already graduated, and if he thinks I'm insane, it can't be held against me—at least, not that I'm aware of—and he is the one who wrote the article, after all.

I tell him everything from the start. He listens without interruption, but he stands and gazes out of the window when I tell him the real reason I'm here.

He hadn't said anything yet, and I begin to wonder if I've pushed the limit.

I watch him like a hawk as he walks back over to his desk, sits down, removes his glasses, and rubs his forehead.

Guess I've given the man a headache or worse.

He stands, pulls out the top drawer of his filing cabinet, removes a file, and hands it to me. "I need to know just how serious you are about this."

"I'm here, aren't I?"

He nods and tells me the information in the file is highly confidential, and I am to read and return it to him intact. He tells me there is a retired science teacher who lives out in Canfield who can help me. He says he leads a group called Orion's Path. A chill runs up my spine when I hear those words again.

Lowry must notice my pallor as he offers me a glass of water. I tell him I need a minute, that it's too much information, and he tells me to sit until I get my bearings.

He pulls up a chair and sits next to me. "So, tell me: how is the state of humanity in 2023?"

I take a deep breath before I speak. "It's a very different world, but we are still here. Technology and artificial intelligence have replaced real, organic professors among other things."

"I was afraid of that," he mumbles. "I needn't know more, for I will not be around to experience it, but my children will, as will the rest of civilization."

I grab his hand, taking the chance he won't pull back, feeling the compassion and empathy the man has for me and mankind. I tell him there is much hope, and many are awakening regarding what our planet needs to survive. I don't mention the pandemic, thinking he has enough to decipher as it is.

He tells me he believes me, but he also reiterates the fact that I cannot divulge any of the information in the folder to anyone. He tells me he expects me to return it to him in two days' time, no excuses.

I rise from my chair, feeling a bit steadier on my feet, and thank him again. I pass by the main office, and the secretary tilts her head to look at me with a disapproving glance, but I don't care. I have a resource now, one that will hopefully explain why I'm here and how to get back home if that's at all possible.

On the drive home, I think about Orion's Path and know that Dylan has been there, but whether he became a member is unbeknownst to me, but I'll continue to do a deeper dive into this for sure.

It seems as if my car is on autopilot once again, as my mind is focused on the folder lying on the passenger's seat instead of driving.

# Chapter 23

I hurry into the house with the folder and hightail it upstairs to my room. Mom is at the store, Dad is at work, and Joe's at a buddy's, working on his Harley. I have some quiet time to myself, and I'm burning daylight. My hands shake as I open the large manilla envelope containing Professor Lowry's papers. There are at least fifty papers in it. Some have been typed on a real typewriter. I've forgotten that's what we used back in the day…this day. There are a few papers with handwritten notes, as well. I want to read them all now, but I know that's not possible. Mom will be home soon, and I want to help her with dinner.

I read the first page that mentions the names of those who contributed to the article. There are several. Professor Lowry's name is mentioned along with the others. The one name that catches my eye is that of Troy Duncan, the founder of Orion's Path. He was a renowned high school science teacher and researcher in time travel, astrology, and meteorology at one time.

*Hmm…meteorology—what did that have to do with all of this?*

I read the next several pages, mentioning famous landmarks from all around the world said to be portals, some of which I've read up on. *I wonder if Mill Creek Park is mentioned in the research, seeing as how the work was mostly done by local scholars.*

My breath catches when I come to the paper on meteorology by Troy Duncan. It mentions portal storms, which are quantum events capable of creating portals, rifts, or tears in space-time at certain locations. These storms could seem like your typical storm, but they affect space-time. They create a high concentration of what is called dechyons, a faster-than-light subatomic particle that interferes with the fabric of space-time that could, indeed, create the perfect portal storm. They are present in the eye of the storm and transmit supercharged matter able to transport a person or object. It said that if one looks into the clouds, one will see the vortex, which resembles lightning jumping around. The portal waves create a glowing blue rain that travels out from the center.

Trying to take in all of this new information has my head spinning. I close my eyes, trying to recall the night of my transport. There were no storms that night, at least, none that I knew of in the area. From what I've read, the storm has to be over the direct location for a time portal to open. Makes sense.

I've always been afraid of lightning, and if I have to travel during a storm, I'd have to be medicated or stoned, for that matter. As a child, I used to hide under the bed whenever we had electrical storms. Even now, I still panic, making sure all of my flashlights are within reach, and spend my time in the inside hallway of my home until the storm has passed. Guess I'd never make a good storm chaser.

I continue to read. It goes into detail on how to make sure a portal storm will be at the desired location for a traveler to enter it. There are several caveats given, as well, one of them being that it's not certain where one might end up, be it advancing several years ahead or regressing further back in time. There is mention of the effects it has on the physical body, one being the aging process. The cellular structure of the body is thrown into a state of shock, and there are accounts of those who age rapidly while others don't age at all.

I sigh at the thought—*oh, to be immortal!* My mind goes to my favorite series, *The Highlander. Maybe Dylan is an Immortal! Maybe he's experienced something like the "quickening."*

*Okay. I have to calm down.*

*Did he behead another Immortal and receive increased powers to be able to do all of this?*

Now I'm thinking crazy. My heart races with all these thoughts. I'd never be able to explain any of it. The only thing I truly know is that my answer likely lies within these papers. There's too much of a connection between Troy Duncan and his so-called science cult.

The garage door opens, and I jam the papers back into the folder, slide it under my pillow, and head downstairs to help Mom carry in the groceries. There'll be time for studying later. My go-go girl costume is all ready for Saturday night. Guess I'll have to check the weather to see if a storm is predicted for that night. I'll have to check the local television channel or the radio broadcast. *Damn—where was a good weather app when you needed it?*

My job as Mom's sous chef is interrupted when Dylan calls. I whisper to Mom that I'll take it upstairs. I race upstairs to take the call on my phone in my room. I wait to hear the click to signify Mom has hung up the kitchen phone before letting Dylan know I'm there.

"Just checking to see if you've picked a place for dinner Saturday night." His voice is riddled with excitement.

"I…I haven't yet."

"You sound tired—everything okay?"

"Yes, yes, I'm just tired. Went job hunting today." I was getting better and better at this lying thing.

"Well, you know you are special to me, and I wanted to let you know that money is no object here. You can pick out the fanciest place in town." His voice is most persuasive.

And it was his voice that got to me again like it always did. Somehow, it chases away all of the frightening cobwebs in my head, the ones that occupied it just a short time ago. He could turn me on with sweet talk alone.

I tell him I'll pick a place by tomorrow. After all, I only have three days left until show time on Saturday night.

He tells me he has a surprise for me, as well, and I wonder what it is. *Is he about to come clean? Is he ready to tell me he's planned this whole caper?*

*Nah. That's just wishful thinking.*

I head downstairs to find that Mom has cut up all of the veggies for the stew, so I set the table. The stew will take a few hours, so we pour ourselves some iced tea and go to sit on the front porch. It's chilly out, but I don't mind. I'd sit out there with her in a blizzard if it meant spending time with her.

She asks how things are going with Dylan, and I tell her that I am looking forward to our date this Saturday. She pries a bit more, asking me if this could turn into something serious.

I tell her I don't know because I really don't, at least not the way things are going now in this realm. What I do know is that it never turned serious back then. I ended up meeting Mark the following week and started dating him while I slowly broke off things with Dylan. *Would that play out the same way this time?* All I know for sure is that I'm stuck here for some odd reason, and I'll try to get back if it's at all possible, but I'll play the game for now.

***

After dinner, I excuse myself, claiming to work on my resume, and head back to my room to finish reading the rest of the papers. I have to return the folder to Professor Lowry tomorrow. If I were smart, I'd have made copies of everything to keep, but I guess I just wasn't thinking. *Mom's office has a copy machine, but what if someone saw me? What if they saw the folder? The professor said that no one was ever to see it.*

I lie on my bed, finishing up the last few pages. One last thing startles me. It mentions what I read in my library research on chanting and music being able to open a portal with sound waves and vibrations. *Maybe it's a combination of all these things?* I'm not sure about that, but I am sure that I'm going to talk to Mr. Troy Duncan about his Orion's Path cult. Maybe he'll be more open to me if I speak with him face to face. Only time will tell, and it looks like I have about forty-some-odd years to go.

# Chapter 24

I can't believe I sleep in on Saturday morning. I have so much to do for tonight. My costume is ready, but I also have an early appointment with the hairdresser. Luckily, she's Mom's neighbor and friend, who owns a local salon. I need a trim, and I want to get a good blowout for tonight. I'm sure the style won't last long with all the sweat I'll produce while performing, but I have to look good for Dylan. More than that, I want to.

I rush downstairs, following the aroma of freshly brewed coffee, and bump into Joe, who's heading upstairs. He's just getting home. He looks hungover and sleepy as I hug him and tell him I hope to see him before tonight.

Mom has saved me a cheese Danish, my favorite. Dad is already dressed and headed outside to mow the lawn. He looks so handsome in his heavy, cable-knit, gray sweater. The mornings are getting cooler, and it's only going to get colder still.

I only have time for one cup of coffee as I'm already running late. My appointment is for 11 a.m. The salon is only fifteen minutes away, but I have to get dressed. I also want to run over to Tracey's for her to suggest makeup ideas for tonight. She's a pro at this and I listen as she offers her best tips on the colors I should wear that will compliment my outfit. She even lets me borrow her glitter eye shadow palette. She tells me that she might be able to do my makeup as well if she doesn't have to babysit for her brother.

There isn't much parking in the salon's lot. I walk in, and MaryAnn is ready for me. She pretty much knows what I want, and we head for the shampoo sinks. Her perfectly styled bob never moves. Guess that's one of the perks of being a hairdresser. She also knows about my date with Dylan. Not much gets past anyone in a small town, let alone in the neighborhood. She asks me about my outfit for tonight, and I freeze. I tell her it's a glittery mini dress—reasoning it's not that far off from the truth.

Glancing in the mirror brings a smile to my face. She's given me the quintessential Farrah Fawcett hairdo.  She gives me a couple of coats of spray—the old-fashioned kind with all the bad stuff that's now banned in my time. I long for the hair gloss serum I have back home and think about the advancements in hair products that have come out since then before paying her, giving her a generous tip, and heading out the door. But no sooner is MaryAnn calling me back in. She tells me that Tracey has called and I'm to head to her house.
I pull out onto Youngstown Poland Road and head for Tracey's house. My excitement builds knowing I'll get a professional-looking makeup session to compliment my new hairdo. It's going to be fun to see what she comes up with.

Tracey and her mom are waiting patiently at the door for me. I wonder if the entire town knows about my date tonight?

Mrs. Blaznick always went out of her way to make me feel at home. She makes us some of her yummy strawberry iced tea and delivers it to her daughter's room.

"I'm so glad I had some time to do this for you. I don't have to watch my brother till later, but I'll still plan on making it up to the club tonight."

Tracey has her enormous makeup case open and ready to go as I peruse over the selection she has. "Why do you have four shades of blue eye shadow?"

"I dunno. Guess I don't want to run out," she says. "You can never have enough shades of blue."

I wonder why the hell we even wore blue back then. I wouldn't be caught dead in it in my sixties.

"You know, you seem different today," she says as she picks up a bottle of light foundation.

"What do you mean?"

"I mean, you aren't all in a fuss with that crazy talk about being from the future."

"Oh…I must be excited about tonight."

"You'd better be excited. I mean, you're gonna be dancing in a cage!"

I hear her loud and clear. *What was I thinking back then? What am I thinking now? And I'm going to repeat the same stupid caper?*

Tracey yells my name twice to snap me out of my trance.

"Yes, we are going to have a blast!"

She instructs me to watch as she applies the winged eyeliner. This is one thing I could never master, but I am no match for her talent.

I thank her for the beautiful job she does and tell her I'll see her at the club.

"Shake it, but don't break it," she tells me as I leave her room.

It's already three, and I need to get home. A sickening feeling arises in my stomach. I know Mom cleans and does laundry every Saturday, and I help her. What if, while I was gone, she found that bikini in my drawer? I try to think back, and I don't remember her ever finding it, so things must still be cool. If she had, I'd surely have some explaining to do.

I think about what Tracey said about me being different as I prep for tonight, having forgotten about time portals and all for the time being. *Have I given up and agreed to stay in the past? It's all very comfortable here.*

*Maybe it's a bit too comfortable. What am I thinking?*

I come to my senses quickly when I think about how time passes, and the fact that I am a prisoner of my past here.

* * *

Dylan is supposed to pick me up early, at 6:30. He's got to help the band set up, and they are the first to play at 7:30. He's on time and looks hot like he always does. Those tight jeans and metallic belt riding low on his hips are going to throw the girls into a real tailspin tonight, not to mention me.

I'll be backstage for a bit before I change into my costume twenty minutes before the band starts. I'm supposed to share a dressing room with another girl. She's Gregg's girlfriend, a new one I haven't met yet. He's been dating her for a few weeks now, from what Dylan tells me.

Dylan escorts me to the dressing room, gives me a quick kiss, and rushes off. I open the door to find a buxom blonde, who appears to be in her late twenties, applying false eyelashes at a dressing table. I walk over to hug her and tell her how we are going to rock it out tonight. I introduce myself, and she tells me her name is Judith. She says she's heard I'm a fantastic dancer, and she's honored to accompany me. From the tone of her voice, she seems to be sincere.

I get up my nerve up to ask her the burning question: "Has Gregg ever mentioned a club called Orion's Path?"

She turns to look at me with one false eyelash dangling off her right lid. "Oh, you mean that stargazing club?"

*I guess that's what he told her it was.*

"Yes, he has. He has gone to a few meetings and wanted me to go, but I couldn't care less about astronomy."

"Yeah, well, I think it's interesting. I mean—"

"That tune we just heard means we'd better get out there," I tell her.

Judith finishes applying her eyelashes and heads out the door.

I check my makeup one more time and shake my head. *I can't believe this is happening again.*

Dylan walks into the dressing room and gives me a passionate kiss, then smacks me on the butt. "You're my witchy woman tonight, babe."

"Ah. So now I know what the first song will be," I tell him.

"I like it as well," he says, smiling, making those dimples more pronounced.

"Oh, you mean the song," I say.

"No, babe. I mean your ass. Gotta run."

"Go do what you do best," I tell him with a slap on his ass.

I take a deep breath as I get myself ready to enter the fray and step into the dimly-lit heart of the seventies club, embracing the impending whirlwind. In an instant, a kaleidoscope of vibrant hues explodes around me, illuminating the steel cage perched on the obsidian platform. *Yes, I'm really going to do this,* I tell myself. It's within those bars that the next hour and a half of my life will unfold. The shadows seem to meld with the hues, enshrouding the very essence of the era in mystery and intrigue. The darkness whispers its secrets, promising a night of enigmatic revelations, ones I still remember well.

The air is alive with anticipation as a throng of people mill about in the electrifying atmosphere. The club pulsates with the melded energies in the room. Amidst the ambient scent of cigarettes and the tang of booze, a symphony of sensations weaves a tapestry of nostalgia. The stage is set for the band's performance, poised on the cusp of unleashing auditory magic upon the crowd.

I cast my gaze over the crowd, adjusting my bikini bottoms with a smile, hopeful for a glimpse of Tracey amidst the dimness, but I don't see any sign of my friend. A sea of unfamiliar faces surrounds me. The darkness provides a veil of anonymity.

The palpable energy of the place is exhilarating. There is a heady mixture of anticipation and raw energy in the room as the band's imminent playtime casts a spell over the crowd, intensifying the intoxicating atmosphere.

As the first notes weave through the air, a familiar melody unfurls—the haunting strains of the Eagles' hit, "Witchy Woman." The rhythm pulses through me, a familiar partner in a dance that has always been one of my favorites. I sway and move, my gaze drawn to Dylan, the captivating frontman commanding the stage. With numerous eyes lingering on me, I remain steadfast, pouring myself into the dance without faltering.

I manage to glance over at Judith, who's in the cage opposite mine, and the music becomes somewhat of an incantation, a conduit for my uninhibited dance.

The band crescendos into Deep Purple's, "Smoke on the Water," igniting the crowd to a fervor. Among the clamor, Tracey's absence causes me concern, but my anticipation remains unshaken. I know what's coming: a climax born from memory but foggy in its exact timing.

About halfway through the song, a collective cry pierces the air: "The pigs are here!"

The ambiance shifts and the crowd hurries toward the exits in a rush of energy. A pair of husky lawmen stand at the entrance, exchanging words with the security guards. The music's melody dwindles to silence, and I seize the moment to slip out of my cage and dart for the refuge of the dressing room. The door closes behind me, cocooning me in safety.

I'm there all by myself and nervous. I want to cut out, but I need to wait for Dylan to take me home. I get up and pace the small room, thinking about my erratic dancing and wondering if he is some sort of witch or wizard who has placed a spell on me to bring me here. I've never acted like that before. I don't recall acting like that when I did my original performance back in the day. *Something is different this time.*

Once again, my mind reverts to the Mandela Effect. *Anything's possible*, I reason.

The door opens, and it's a cop, a younger one, whose face bears a few scars. He approaches and asks for my ID or driver's license.

I open my purse and pull out my wallet.

He glances at my license and my name, looks up at me, and says, "You related to the mayor?"

"Uh…he's my uncle. My dad's brother," I say in a shaky voice. I tell him I'm with the band. He nods his head to show he understands, and I feel as if I can breathe again.

"Go home, young lady, and think twice about performing in places like this," he says. "I know you come from a good family. You need to start making better choices."

Though Uncle Bob's clout gets me off this time, I pray the cop won't tell him or my parents.

Dylan finally comes into the room, seeming as cool as a cucumber. "You okay?"

"If not for my uncle, I guess I'd be spending the night in the pokey."

"Oh, a cop questioned you?"

"Uh-huh. Guess he thought I was underage."

"Helps if the mayor's your uncle." He laughs.

"Not funny. Why were the cops here, anyway?" I ask, my eyes on the door, ready to book if another cop comes in.

"Just checking for underage drinkers and possibly minor betting. Happens here a lot," he explains.

I shake my head and grab my jacket, ready to go home.

We pull into the driveway, and I realize I'm still in my bikini under my short jacket. I know sometimes Mom waits up for me eager to hear about my night. It's not long enough to cover up my costume, but I've left my change of clothes back at the club.

*Damn!*

Dylan offers to go back, but I say no. I don't want to go anywhere near that place.

"So, where *do* you want to go?"

"Let's go to your apartment," I say without hesitation.

"You serious?"

"Serious," I say.

I know it's not planned, but I'll think of a good explanation tomorrow. Right now, I just want to be with him, and badly.

# Chapter 25

It seems as if we've flown to Dylan's apartment complex, which should usually take about a half-hour drive from the club. *Is that also one of his supernatural powers? That is, if he has any. Maybe it's just because he's as horny as I am.*

We can't get in the door fast enough. Once inside, he informs me that Gregg is spending the night with Judith, so we have free reign of the apartment.

Dylan pins me against the wall in the entryway next to the large mirror and thrusts his hard body against mine, our tongues entangled in an erotic dance. He removes my tasseled top and massages my breasts. I throw my head back and moan in delight, calling out, "Yes, yes!"

My body responds to his touch. Already aroused, I'm quick to check on his shielded member in those tight jeans. He's quite hard, and his bulge is about ready to burst through.

He whispers in my ear to follow him into his bedroom, where he removes my bottoms and flings them onto the floor. He undresses at light speed and pushes me down onto the black and white checkered comforter, eager to mount me.

"Do you want me?" he asks seductively.

"I want all of you," I whisper into his ear.

He reaches for a condom in the bedside table drawer, slips it on, and enters me slowly, pulling out only to thrust his hardness into me again with greater intention. "I want you so bad," I say into his ear with a moan.

He squeezes my butt cheeks and tells me he loves my hard ass as I'm about ready to come.

We come together, then lie exhausted on the bed. He rolls over and asks me to spend the night.

I have only one answer, that being a "yes." I guess I'll have to come up with a pretty good excuse for my overnight absence, even though I'm well over twenty-one, after all.

It's good to take a hot shower with him. It relaxes me, especially after all the drama at the club tonight.

We towel off and slip into bed naked. I have no pajamas, given the fact that I hadn't planned on spending the night.

I am antsy, and so is Dylan. It's not until 2 a.m., and we're both still awake that I find the courage to ask him about Orion's Path.

He hesitates, and I wait impatiently for a response. "Oh, yeah. You remember me telling you that Gregg was going to meetings there, and he wanted me to join. He's into all this astrology shit, and he thinks I'll like it, too."

"Maybe I'll join you one of these nights," I say.

"Oh. It's my understanding that it's a men's only club."

I respond, "You don't say," but I'm not satisfied with that and try to push it further. "So, you're telling me it's a sexist organization? I mean, women are interested in science, too."

He fumbles for words. "Not my rules, babe. It's the club's policy."

*Now, I know there's something here, something that jives with the information in the folder from Professor Lowry. I'll have to find a way to sneak into that club soon, but for now, I try to enjoy the moment and have faith that I'm right where I'm supposed to be at this moment in time.*

I rise while it's still dark and look at my watch. It's only 5:30. I can only imagine how worried my folks are will be when they find my bed still made. Dylan is still asleep, so I throw on my jacket and make my way to the kitchen to use the phone, knowing Mom will be up early. She always was an early riser.

I call her at six and tell her I'm with Tracey, and the band had to stay late at the club, so she drove me to her house, and we decided to make it a girls' night. I tell her I'll be home later this morning.

The call ends, and the realization hits me again that I still don't have a change of clothes. I'll have to think quickly to remedy the situation, but I need some coffee in my system first, so I rummage through the old oak cupboards in the kitchen and find some. I brew a pot, thinking Dylan will want some, too.

*Guess it's too much to ask for cream and sugar.* But I reason if there's none I'll go without.

I do another search and find a small ceramic sugar bowl and a carton of milk in the fridge next to a six-pack of beer.

An hour later, I call Tracey to invite myself over to her house. I tell her I'll explain everything when I get there. I'll have Dylan drive me. She tells me no worries, that she's just glad I'm safe. I know she'll let me borrow something from her closet, even though she's two sizes bigger than me.

Now, I just need to come up with an excuse as to why I'm wearing new digs. Mom knows every piece of clothing I own. Regardless, it's probably an easier excuse to conger than trying to explain why I was out all night with a musician.

Of course, Tracey is at the door, patiently waiting for me, still wearing her red bathrobe. Dylan kisses me and peels out of the driveway.

I run to the door, as it's freezing, hug her, and tell her she's the best friend ever.

Luckily, her parents and her little brother are at church for early mass, so it's just the two of us. She looks me over, notices that I'm still in my costume, and raises an eyebrow. "You need some clothes, lady."

I follow her into her room. She opens up a drawer, throws a pair of jeans on the bed, and comes out of her closet with a long-sleeved white blouse.

"Guess it'll have to do," I tell her.

"Better than showing up at home in that getup!" she chuckles.

We both have a good laugh. I need that.

She asks if I've had breakfast, and I tell her I'm starving. She makes us scrambled eggs and toast, and we sit in the dining room to eat.

"Well? Come on—spill the beans, girlfriend!"

"First, let me ask what happened to you last night. I mean, it was crazy," I say.

"I saw the cop cars as I was about to pull into the club and decided it wasn't the best idea," she says, pouring herself another cup of coffee.

"Tell me about it! It was nuts! I mean, a cop came into my dressing room, asked me for my driver's license, and then asked if I was related to Mayor Kovich."

Tracey about drops her cup. "What happened then?"

"He told me to go home and think twice about performing in places like that."

"You know, I heard that place was owned by a mobster, maybe one of the biggest ones in Youngstown," Tracey adds.

"Yeah, and we know he's got a monopoly on places like that."

Tracey asks me how my dancing was going until we were raided. I tell her that I was on fire, and I was. I didn't remember ever moving like that before with my previous performance. It must have been the music that brought it out of me—again.

She questions me about the rest of my night, and like the best girlfriend ever, I tell her, not leaving out any details.

"You know, lady? You, like, made history! That is so cool! Just think about how you'll look back on this someday and have something to tell your children or grandchildren."

"Ugh… maybe not." I laugh.

*I made history, all right, and I'm reliving it again. I won't bring up any of the time travel stuff, knowing the point is most likely moot where Tracey is concerned.*

I pick up the phone to tell Mom I'll be home shortly. There is no answer. I figure they are probably still at church.

*Boom! Another stroke of luck. I still have time to change out of Tracey's clothes before they get home.*

Talking about luck, I hope I'll find the time to make my way over to Orion's Path sometime on Monday after I return the file to the professor. I know I'm getting closer to finding the truth of how I arrived here.

# Chapter 26

*Dylan*

I don't know why it amazes me that I was able to play every song without one slip-up last night. All was right on key. As told, everything is just as it was back in 2023. It was so good to be back with the band again. I've really missed these guys. Seeing Dale alive has me taken aback, and I need to take a few deep breaths when every time I see him. *If I could only convince him to change his lifestyle now, but I know playing with time can have repercussions, and I don't need any more drama.*

The guys and I have a practice session later today. We need to discuss if we'll ever perform at the Stardust Room again. I mean, we were only halfway through our first session when the police came. The people who paid to see us play had to leave after the bust. As I recall, we decided to dump that joint.

My thoughts turn to Jenn. She was absolutely terrified she'd be arrested. I feel bad she had to relive that part again.

My mind races back to last night and her dancing up in the cage. She was a real natural. The way she twisted and moved her body to the music was pure magic. Simply thinking about it makes me horny. She always told me she'd dance for me, hoping to turn me on, but she also had that effect on every other male watching her. *I wonder if it even dawned on her how she was able to perform so well and without inhibitions. Did acting out her moves differently somehow lead her to become more suspicious?* There was no way in hell she'd remember every move she made that first time. Did she know more than she was letting on?

I also wonder if she'll continue to pursue her investigation into why she was thrust back here. I think I'm doing a pretty good job of playing clueless. She seems happy, and our attraction to each other is purely electric, not to mention the sex.

There is no one else I can turn to for help or confide in about this supernatural experience, not even Troy Duncan—he'd made that crystal clear before I left in 2023. I'm on my own here, and I have to make damn sure she stays put. Of course, I'd never hurt her or stand in her way if she wants to leave. I've thought about having Gregg follow her, but for what reason? Not to mention that if she caught on, it'd be over.

Troy told me I would never be able to return to 2023, but if Jenn found the means, she would actually go?

I need to stop this incessant worrying because that would be almost impossible for her. I convince myself it will never happen and that I should simply enjoy being back where I've longed to be for some time now. I've spent two years at that cult, learning and preparing.

Now and then, my mind flashes back to the night guard I attacked. I hope he's all right. There's no way of finding, seeing that he won't even begin working at the club until some forty-seven years in the future. That was the first and only time I've ever committed a crime— did bringing Jenn back count? That in itself could flat-out be construed as a case of kidnapping.

# Chapter 27

Time is going by so fast.

I look at the big calendar hanging by the fridge. It's open to a beautiful page, with the October header surrounded by large, colorful oaks and a photo of a covered bridge that's not far from here. I have to admit I really love the change of seasons, not to mention the cooler weather. It seems as if the weather in Florida never cools off until late November. I even used to toy with the idea of moving back after retirement but never had the energy.

I stuff everything back into the folder to return to Professor Lowry's office today. Mom and Dad have already gone to work by the time I manage to get dressed and head downstairs. Joe's door is closed—I assume he's still asleep.

Feeling anxious, I head over to grab a coffee at the university coffee shop. I'll need the caffeine boost if I'm going to see the professor again. My pulse is already racing at the mere thought of it.

Out of habit, I glance down at my wrist, looking for the smartwatch to check out my heart rate.

*Oh, how I miss some of those modern conveniences now.*

I pull the belt tighter on my jacket, head toward the science center, and enter through the main hall. The same snooty secretary glances up at me as I approach the desk. I tell her I'm here to see the professor. She tells me to have a seat as he is running behind. I take a seat on the wooden bench and try to keep my breathing slow and steady.

The main doors open, and I am shocked to see Paul, that handsome student, walk in. He heads in my direction and takes a seat next to me.

I turn to him and ask, "Are you stalking me?"

He laughs, although I don't find it amusing in the least. "I'm not stalking you, Jennifer."

*He remembers my name? Damn, that's creepy.*

"So, why are you here?"

"I'm actually here to see you," he says, in a friendly manner.

"What? Why? What do you want?" I'm on the defensive now.

"Look, I need to come clean with you. I'm a TA for Professor Lowry. I'm on his research team. He contacted me last week and told me all the details of your dilemma."

I think I'm in shock. I feel violated. Paul must notice the physical signs because he asks, "Are you alright?"

I take some deep breaths. "I don't know. Honestly. I—"

"It's okay," he says softly, and he takes my hand. "I'm on your side. Here to help."

I feel a small electrical shock when he touches me. "How could you possibly—"

The secretary stands and tells us the professor will see us now.

I shudder and rub my hand where I felt the shock.

The professor greets us at the door. He doesn't smile as he invites us to enter and have a seat.

Paul and I sit across from the large metal desk.

I set the folder on his desk and thank him.

He asks me if it was at all helpful. I tell him it was, indeed, more than I had expected.

"I see you've met Paul," he says, his chin jutting in Paul's direction.

"Yes, I have."

"He's been my protégé for a few years now. Going to make a wonderful science professor someday," he says proudly.

"I don't really care what the hell he is or becomes. I'm at the point now where I want answers to all of this…this fucking game, if that's what it is!" I shout. "Am I a part of some dark experiment of yours?"

"Not at all, Miss Kovich. Why on earth would you even think such a thing?" the professor asks. "You came to us, remember."

I shake my head. "I'm sorry. I just need answers. I need help."

*God, I sound pathetic.*

"That's why I've asked Paul to intercede for you. He's got connections with Orion's Path, and he knows Troy Duncan."

"Are you telling me he's a member of that cult?"

Paul turns to me. "Not quite. I'm there, but for research only. I'm doing my thesis on quantum physics and time travel."

*I find it all so incredibly convenient, but hey, I'll listen to anything if it will get me back to my time period.*

Paul continues, "I've had a couple of sessions there and was invited to another one, one that not every member is privy to. I've come to find out there's a dark side to Troy's experiments."

*I should have seen it coming. I've read my share of paranormal novels, especially ones with dark cults. How could I have been so naive?*

He tells me that Orion's Path is a front for what's really going on there. He goes on to tell me there's a secret room in the basement that houses a makeshift lab where a few selected individuals practice ancient magic to achieve out-of-body experiences and experiment with time travel.

"So, exactly what is our plan here, gentlemen?" I look from Paul to the professor and back again, hoping I won't develop whiplash.

"Paul will take you to a session for new members. He will speak to Troy, telling him you have an interest in this sort of thing."

I listen intently and ask, "And then what? What can Troy do for me?"

The professor stands. "Paul will convince Troy to help you return to your time period using the portal method once you have gained his trust."

"What does he get in return? I don't have millions of dollars here."

"Don't be silly," the professor states. "It's all in the name of research. In fact, you'll be helping us."

"By using dark magic? I'm not into that sort of thing. I don't plan on selling my soul to the devil."

"That's not the plan," the professor states. "Just to let you know, I'll be far removed from all of this. I can't get involved in any of this, or my career would be on the line. This is where Paul comes in."

"So, tell me: will there be black robes and a sacrifice?"

"Not quite, but there *will* be a ritual. Not like any of the ones you've seen in films," Paul says as if it's going to make me feel any better about any of this.

I get up from my chair and walk over to the window, buying time as I decide if I want to partake in this madness. *It may be the only option I have to get home—what can it hurt?* I reason.

Paul informs me that once we are squared away with my visit to Orion's Path, and I feel comfortable with my role, all we'll need to do is wait for the perfect storm.

"Ah. The perfect storm, huh? Guess that's the one that opens up the portal. *I wonder if I'll be like Dorothy in **The Wizard of Oz** and end up in the Emerald City.*" He did say dark magic—maybe there will be a wicked witch or two; God help me.*

I walk back and plop down in the hard wooden chair. "I'm in, then."

Paul informs me that he will contact me after he speaks to Troy Duncan.

I pick up my purse and turn to Paul, "So, I guess it's a date, then?"

He takes my hand. "It's a date."

*A date with the devil, I presume.*

I feel that electrical shock again. It's not a surge but something different. Oddly enough, it feels good this time. I rub my wrist, and the feeling fades.

Professor Lowry says, "This is the last time you will have contact with me."

I have a few hours to spare before heading home. I decide to head back over to Mill Creek Park and Lanterman's Mill. If it's a portal, it might be just the ticket I need.

There are a handful of cars in the parking lot. I didn't expect it to be crowded for a Monday. The afternoon has warmed up, so I leave my jacket in the car and head toward the mill, hoping to speak with the caretaker. *It couldn't hurt—right?* I'm not placing all of my eggs in the professor and Paul's basket. I walk around to the backside of the mill, facing the creek. Something tells me to sit right here and listen to the water as it trickles down the creek. There is something so soothing about the sound of running water. I get that sleepy feeling again, so I close my eyes and lie on the soft grass.

The breeze picks up, ushering in a strange kind of energy, one that makes me feel as if I've been here before. A strong sense of deja vu encompasses me as the musky smell of the tall oaks and hemlocks engulf my nose.

A couple strolling by wakes me out of my trance. They are young lovers who stop and make out at the end of the path. I stare and watch them as they continue the passionate embrace. I sigh, *Some people do lead normal lives.*

After a brief moment of feeling sorry for myself, I walk back over to the millhouse. The door to the museum is open, but there is no caretaker there and no visitors. I use my time to check out the gift shop, perusing the mementos, stuffed animals, postcards, and the like. Though nothing calls out to me, I buy a bronze coin with the mill's logo on it, dated 1820. I also purchase a small booklet on the mill's history, yearning once more for my smartphone. I'm hoping maybe there will be something in the booklet that will lead to more clues regarding this place being a portal. Then again, if there are, I seriously doubt they'd reveal it to the public. *Why are these things always kept so secretive?*

# Chapter 28

It's been a pretty quiet day. Mom and Dad are working, and Joe's over at his buddy's house, working on some bikes. I'm supposed to meet Paul at the Stronger Brew Coffee Shop in an hour, but I'm not sure how he'll be able to arrange a meeting with Troy and me so quickly. I'm still not sure if I trust him. Something is off, but I can't dismiss anything now, especially when I'm so close to getting some clues about how to get back home.

I can't help but stare at the framed picture of Mom and Dad that sits on my dresser as I open the bottom drawer and pull out a long-sleeved red top. *How many times have I wished that I could spend just ten more minutes with them? Yet here I am, with the chance to spend days with them. Instead, every one of those days is being spent looking for a way back to my time, and for what?*

I shake my head and look up at the ceiling. *I know I'm being tested. I seriously do need to get back to church.*

I pull on my top, brush my long hair, secure it into a high ponytail, and throw on a pair of jeans.

Once again, it seems as if the old Road Runner knows its way around town. It's about a twenty-five-minute drive to the coffee shop. I slip in an Emerson, Lake, and Palmer eight-track to try and calm my nerves. I anticipate Paul will be on time. He seemed to have been overly excited to escort me to see Troy.

I pull into the back parking lot next to a small convertible MG. Paul had told me what he'd be driving. The place is pretty empty for 2 p.m. Guess the lunch rush has already cleared out.

Paul is seated at a back table with a cup which I assume to be coffee. He's wearing a jean jacket, and his coal-black hair is tucked behind his ears, revealing a small diamond earring in his right earlobe. He could probably pass for a rocker himself. He doesn't quite fit the bill of the quintessential astrology student.

He asks me what I'd like to drink, and I tell him a hot black tea would be great, but I don't know if the caffeine will help settle my nerves or send me into overdrive. I wait while he walks over to the counter to put in my order, thinking about how much coffee shops have changed over the years. This place is nothing like Starbucks.

"So, are you ready to meet Troy?" he asks upon returning with my tea.

"I guess. I mean—"

"You have nothing to worry about," he says, sensing my nervousness. "I've told him I'm bringing in a friend of mine who is a guest and interested in astrology."

"Oh," I say, reaching for my tea. "I'm sure that excited him." I have a vision of this Troy guy resembling Darth Vader.

He goes on to tell me to play the part. "Just pretend you have an interest in astrology and time portals. Tell him you plan on writing a novel on it, possibly a fiction novel. We have to ease our way in."

I get goosebumps wondering how he could possibly know that I was a writer. Had *I told him that earlier? Can he read minds, too?*

My fingers tap against the small wooden table.

Paul notices my nervousness. "Listen, Jennifer, I want to help you."

"What do you get from all of this?" I ask, watching his facial movements closely.

"As I've already said, I hope to gain some information for myself. Anything we learn will benefit the both of us." He reaches out to touch my arm. "I've told you I will add this to my ongoing research."

Once again, I feel a little shock when he touches me, and I pull back.

"You okay?"

"Guess you don't believe in fabric softener," I say.

He laughs. "Seems I have that effect on some people. I think it's just static." He tugs at his jacket. "Never been too good at laundry."

I sip my tea as Paul checks his watch. "We need to leave here soon. I told Troy we'd be there at three. By the way, I believe there might be a few others at the orientation as well."

*Hmm…more infiltrators. Will they be science nerds or innocent victims?*

We drive through the back roads of Canfield until we come to a long gravel driveway and approach the two-story, log-style cabin. There are a few other cars parked in the adjacent gravel parking lot to the side.

Paul taps me on the shoulder. "You got this, Jenn."

I take a deep breath and nod. I never was much of an actress, having dropped out of drama club only after a few months of high school.

A tall, blond man greets us at the door. His hair is tied back with a leather hair tie. His face holds echoes of a hard lifestyle.

Paul introduces me to Troy, who appears to be in his late thirties. He reaches his hand out to me. "It's good to have you here. We will be starting one of our introductory meetings in about fifteen minutes. Paul tells me you are interested in astrology. We don't usually get into the meat of the methodology until members have completed the first few sessions and are vetted. I'm sure Paul has told you until recently we've only been admitting males but I've made some exceptions lately, that is if you are truly interested in becoming a member."

"By the way, please help yourself to coffee or tea in the kitchen."

*I have the urge to slap this sexist pig right in the jaw, but then I reason I'm going to need him.*

I glance around at the high-beamed ceilings and interesting Navajo rugs hanging throughout the spacious loft area. *This is no rinky-dink cult here. Someone's put some cash into the place.*

Troy excuses himself, and Paul leads me into the kitchen area to get some tea. He obviously knows his way around the place. I must get myself collected. I'm here to gain respect from Troy and maybe learn a few things. I'm putting all of my trust in Paul, as well, and I'm still not sure about this Troy dude. I have no idea what lies ahead of me. I'm preparing myself to be inducted into some dark demonic cult, based on what I've heard so far.

We are escorted into a large living room area set up with a few rows of wooden folding chairs. A fire crackles in a stone fireplace on the far wall. A handful of young people take a seat on the opposite side of the aisle.

Troy approaches the podium. There's a large projector screen behind him for the presentation, I assume. They have no idea how easier life will be in the future with PowerPoint.

Futuristic music begins to play, and the screen is illuminated with geometric symbols, constellations, and other scientific symbols. *Damn—I wish I paid more attention in science class.*

All is quiet as the slide show ends, and Troy clears his throat. "I welcome all of you here today. It does my heart good to know we continue to have those who are interested and open to new science and the technology it has to offer."

*I have to hold my tongue. This is 1976, for God's sake. If he lives long enough, he will see what new technology awaits him.* I quiet my mind and try to listen.

Troy quotes famous scientists such as Ptolemy, Galileo, Einstein, Nikolai Kozyrev, and Johannes Kepler. He even mentions HG Wells. I've heard of them all except for Nikolai Kozyrev. *Guess I'll need to do some research to get myself up to speed. If I only had my iPhone with me.*

He tells us we will be studying many of their theories on astronomy and time travel, and I wonder if he has a time machine hidden somewhere on the grounds.

After the six of us introduce ourselves, he distributes a syllabus with the information for the next three meetings. *Geez, I feel like I'm back in college again. Then again, he was a high school teacher, after all.*

I glance over the papers and wonder if I'll even be around long enough to attend. Hopefully, Paul will have the answers to get me back, so I won't have to spend any more time here than necessary.

* * *

I'm quiet on the drive home, which Paul is quick to notice. "What's wrong, Jenn?"

*He's got to be kidding me.* I can list a slew of things that are wrong, but I give him a simple yet honest answer. "I just don't know. I mean, it's been at least three weeks now, and I'm still here. And now I'll have to attend all of these meetings to gain more information."

Paul takes his eyes off the road for a second and turns to face me. "Look, Jenn, not at all. I've been attending meetings here for the past four months, and I want Troy to trust you and myself as well. He doesn't know I'm here under false pretenses. I can tell you that I know more than Troy Duncan on this subject."

"Then why are we here?" I ask, with an incredulous look. "Why do we even need him?"

"He's got some machines and high-tech equipment here, plus he's privy to a few spells used by those famous scientists he mentioned. He's got quite a private collection of old books he bought years ago that contain some powerful experiments as well."

"Ah, so now we're digging deep into the dark side?" I shake my head and gaze out the window.

"Uh, sort of. I know what to be careful of, so you don't need to worry," he says as if trying to ease my nerves.

I ask him about that Kozyrev guy, and he tells me he was a Russian physicist who invented a prototype for a time machine using a type of concave mirror that was later made famous, coined the "Kozyrev Mirror," used in makeshift time travel machines. He says Kozyrev knew a lot about time travel and was said to have experienced it himself.

*Now, I have visions of myself sitting in a time machine just like the guy did in one of H.G. Well's movies. It didn't end well for him.*

It's late when we get back to the coffee shop, which has already closed. I thank Paul and tell him how grateful I am for all of his help. He tells me he'll pick me up next week for the second meeting.

I can't stop thinking about Paul and Troy all the way home. Too many thoughts run through my head. *How did I ever end up in this weird dilemma?*

Mom and Dad's car is in the garage when I pull in. I don't see Joe's bike.

I walk into the house minus the handouts from the meeting. I'd be up well past midnight if I had to explain why I attended a cult meeting, let alone a dark one.

Mom hugs me and tells me there's a plate of lasagna in the fridge and that Dylan has called.

With everything that went on today, I decide to eat first before returning Dylan's call. I'll need the extra energy. I hate hiding things from him, but I can't shake the feeling that he's hiding something even bigger from me.

# Chapter 29

Mom's lasagna is as delicious as it always was. She sits with me while I eat, and we talk about taking a trip down to Volant Mills in Pennsylvania this weekend. We always enjoy all of the little shops filled with handmade items and special foods in the quaint Amish town. It's been a sort of ritual for us since my teens.

I tell her I'm in. It'll be a good distraction for me.

I excuse myself, knowing I need to go upstairs to call Dylan. I have so many mixed emotions running through me, some that worry me and others that make me tingle. I think back to the sex the other night. It was damn good, and I want to have it again.

I'm about to hang up after the fourth ring, but he picks up, his voice is riddled with excitement. "Hey, babe. Got an invite to a huge house party in Boardman. It's the drummer's house from Velvet Thunder. Going to be the party of the year, and I want to show you off to my friends."

"As long as I don't have to dance in a cage again."

Dylan laughs and tells me I'll have the night off but that I should plan to wear something sexy.

I accept his offer, and he tells me he'll pick me up on Saturday at 7 p.m.

That means I'll need to get in touch with Paul to see if he has any instructions for me. I feel as if I'm cheating now. It seems I've somehow been bestowed with a gift for pathological lying. I do have to admit that he's easy on the eyes with those striking, dark features of his.

It's almost sunset when I head out to the front porch as Mom tidies up in the kitchen. I walk alongside her pristine flowerbed, filled with a colorful assortment of flowers. She always had a knack for this. I run my hand along the petals of the vibrant purple pansies and brilliant marigolds that feel like soft velvet against my skin. Now that October is here, I know they won't last, but hey, nothing lasts forever.

Before turning in, I glance inside my closet, searching for something sexy as Dylan had suggested, pull out a dark green, low-cut mini dress, and hold it up against myself as I glance in the mirror. It compliments my strawberry-blonde hair. Red and green—*how can you go wrong with Christmas colors?*

I'm not that tired when I finally turn in, wondering if Brandy has been looking for me. What about Laney? I miss my daughter and wonder if I'll ever see her again, but if I'm stuck in this realm, I'll give birth to her in five years if I'm still around. I'd have to marry Mark first, though. This is making my head spin. It would have made for a great *Twilight Zone* episode. I close my eyes, hoping, once again, that this is just a bad dream and I'll wake up back home tomorrow, but when tomorrow arrives, I'm still in my pink and green bedroom back in 1976.

Right after breakfast, I call Paul, who tells me he'll call Troy to see if he can arrange a private meeting before the weekend. He says he'll call me as soon as he knows something.

I wonder again how this is all possible. *How can Troy trust us and agree to help me when I've been brought in as a possible new member? Paul will have to come clean with him, and I'm not sure how that will pan out. Either way, I'm skeptical.*

My mind races back to my research from the library, and I have to question myself if this is all worth it. It might be dangerous, but I don't think I have the ability to return to 2023 on my own. I realize that I need Paul and possibly Troy, both of whom I still don't trust, but I have no choice. And Professor Lowry is totally out of the question. He'd made that crystal clear during our meeting.

The house is quiet. Mom and Dad have gone to work. I want to call Tracey, but I know she's already at work. We have a date to drive up to Kent State next weekend to go to some of the popular clubs. They have some of the best live bands there. If I have my dates right, that is the night I will meet Mark. *If I decide not to go, would that change the course of history?* I could still go but refuse his offer to dance. If I do, it would mean we wouldn't get into a relationship sometime in the future.

*Ugh! All of this time travel crap is making me dizzy.*

Paul's call interrupts my reverie. He tells me that we do, indeed, have a private meeting with Troy tomorrow afternoon.

My Spidey sense kicks into action, and I voice my safety concerns to Paul.

He assures me all is good, and he tells me to meet him at the coffee shop tomorrow at 2 p.m. sharp.

Both of these men seem to be quick to come to my rescue. Dark thoughts seep into my mind. *Could this be some kind of a trap?*

I leave the house at 1:30. It's easy to slip out because I don't have to make up any excuses for my whereabouts. Mom asks me what I have planned for this week, and I tell her I'll most likely be applying for jobs.

That's when the thought hits me: I have to drop off my resume at a few more district offices. I'm sure one of them will call soon to offer me a substitute position after they've vetted my resume. I pray I'm outta Dodge before then.

I pull into the parking lot, spot Paul's car, and park right next to the green MG convertible. There are a handful of cars here—I figured it wouldn't be crowded, being that it's too late for lunch.

Paul is at a back table again, and I head his way. He has a huge grin on his face, and I wonder what he's got planned this time. I can only imagine.

He takes my hand, tells me how good it is to see me, and compliments me on the gold blazer I have on. He's already ordered a cup of coffee for himself, and he asks me if I'd like a hot tea. *Seems he remembered that from the last time.*

I'm anxious to hear about his plan, tapping my foot as I wait for him to return from the counter with my tea. In those tight-fitting jeans and a black leather jacket, I can't help but admire his sexy backside.

My tea is too hot to drink, so I blow on it and get right into querying Paul. "So, tell me: what's this new plan of yours?"

"I know the clock is ticking for you, but I have most of the research I need. You said you have an upcoming date with Dylan and you can possibly quiz him for more answers to see if he is involved, but the more I think of it, I believe he may be under some sort of spell and unable to help you in your predicament."

*Hmm, I have to wonder about that one.*

"The sooner we figure this out, the sooner you'll be on your way home. What I need is to convince Troy that you would be a good test subject for his latest time travel method. That means being honest about all the details of your story if you want it to work."

"You think he'll go for that?" I ask.

"Not sure, but we have to give it a try. I mean, what do you have to lose?"

"I don't know…what if I end up in some prehistoric world or on a distant planet?"

Paul laughs. The dimple in his chin is more pronounced, making him even more attractive. "Not gonna happen. I'm taking precautions. I've put extensive safety measures into place, but there are always going to be risks. You've no doubt read about that in your own research. Nothing is foolproof."

"Yeah, like returning and aging rapidly or having some medical malady."

He grins. "Let's hope for the best. You do know you have a choice."

I think about that for a moment. *Seriously, what are the chances I'll end up going back but looking like Grandma Moses or worse?* I shrug my shoulders. "So, tell me: do you think I'll have to sit in one of those huge, clunky time machines?"

"Not sure, but he told me he has a few smaller makeshift ones in the basement. Claims he hasn't used them in a while, though."

I feel my eyes widen. *What the hell am I getting into?*

"There are other methods of time travel, ones that don't require a machine. I think you mentioned reading about the portal method in your studies."

"Yes, and it's really interesting." I go on to tell him about Lanterman's Mill possibly being such a portal.

He nods his head. "Yes, I've done a bit of research on that place myself. There's not much information there, but we can't rule it out in case Troy's plan doesn't work."

Paul informs me that it's time to get going, so I ask for a to-go cup for my tea, and we head out to his car. The afternoon air has gotten colder, and I pull my blazer tighter around me for warmth.

As we drive through the picturesque countryside, I gaze at the leaves on the trees, some of which are just beginning to turn color. I have missed this since moving to Florida.

When we pull into the back parking lot, we're the only car there, making the situation seem even creepier than it already is. I turn to Paul before opening the door. "Just to let you know, if he even suggests any dark magic shit, I'm outta here. I know that's bad stuff, and I don't want any part of it."

Paul takes my hand. "Not to worry. I won't let that happen."

I squeeze his hand and let out a big sigh, feeling another light shock, but I don't flinch this time. I guess I've gotten used to it. *I do need to do a deeper dive into this whole tingly, shocking thing, but not at this time. I've got bigger fish to fry.*

We walk side by side up to the front door, where Troy's muscular henchman greets us and escorts us over to meet him in the main hall. *I feel as if I'm heading into Frankenstein's laboratory; God help me.*

# Chapter 30

Paul and I both decline the refreshments offered by a tall, balding middle-aged man. I wonder if he's a member or another one of Troy's henchmen. I don't know about Paul, but I'll be damned if I'll drink the Kool-Aid here. Paul tells Troy this is an urgent matter, one he'll be most interested in.

I follow Troy with Paul behind me as we enter the main meeting hall. The folding chairs are stacked up against the back wall. Troy sits on what appears to be an antique-style loveseat at the front of the room and motions for us to take a seat on the matching blue sofa across from him. There's an oak coffee table in the middle with a few old books stacked on it, as well as Orion's Path pamphlets. The sunlight from the large bay window streams golden sunlight into the room which highlights the deep facial lines on Troy's face. He gets up to pull the drapes closed, which has me wondering about the dark secrets he's trying to keep in.

My stomach does flip-flops just imagining what will be said and how the conversation will turn out.

Troy returns to the loveseat, tilts his head, and fixes his gaze upon Paul. "So, tell me, Paul: Why the urgency in this meeting?"

Paul clears his throat and tells Troy about my experience from the very beginning. He leaves out no details.

Troy seems to listen intently. He nods his head, and I get the impression he's heard stories similar to mine.

Paul finishes, and Troy stands and walks toward the now-draped window. He turns to face Paul. "I think what bothers me most is the fact that you brought this young lady here under false pretenses." His eyebrows knit together. "All of our possible members take an oath of truth and secrecy to protect the organization."

"Yes, but I figured that, given all your knowledge, you'd be able to help us out," Paul says.

"What do you know of my knowledge?" he asks Paul.

"Not only have I attended several of your meetings, but I've done my own research. I've read up on you, and you do have quite the following. It's impressive." Paul watches Troy's facial movements, hoping that flattery will get him to trust him and Jenn.

Troy sits back down. "What part do I play in all of this?"

"You can help Jenn get back home. She doesn't belong here. If anyone understands, I know it's you," Paul says, his finger pointing to Troy,

"This rocker guy, Dylan, that you speak of…he was here for one meeting with his friend, Gregg, his band's drummer, but it's been a while."

My ears perk up when Troy mentions Dylan's name. "Is he behind all this?"

"I can't really say. He didn't seem too interested in what we do here, but I can't say the same for his friend."

*Is Gregg the one into all this shit? Maybe Gregg's the one behind all this*, I wonder.

Paul stands again, pacing the floor behind the sofa. He shakes his head a few times and looks over at us as we wait patiently for a response.

Troy walks over and sits next to me. "I'm sorry this happened to you, but I can't guarantee my methods will take you back. I've studied this science for fifteen years now and have built experimental machines trying to achieve time travel. If we are to move forward, you've got to know there are risks involved."

I nod my head and feel a trickle of tears fall down my cheeks. "I've done some research, and yes, I am aware of the risks. I'm willing to go for it, nevertheless."

"You know this poses a risk for me, too, Miss Kovich, should I decide to help you in this endeavor."

Paul stands and turns toward Troy, hands on his hips. "What, exactly, would those risks be, might I ask?"

"My reputation, for fuck's sake!" Troy yells, throwing up his hands in the air.

Paul shakes his head. "You've already built quite a large following, and you maintain a credible stance in the field of science among the locals here."

"Yes, the locals, indeed, and in a positive one, and I intend to keep it that way. And for the record, I'm pushing to win a grant I recently applied for and move my lab up into Mt. Shasta in California. If I win that grant, I will become even more well-known in the world of science, taking my work to a wider audience—perhaps internationally."

Paul listens intently, then asks, "What, exactly, are you afraid of here? I mean, you've been known to take risks like this before."

Troy paces again, then says, "Let me tell you, Miss Kovich, you have no idea what or whom you are dealing with here."

A middle-aged, muscular man enters the room, no doubt prompted by his booming voice. "Everything okay?" asks the henchman, who's dressed in all black.

"It's all good," Troy says, motioning with his hand for him to leave the room.

We are all sitting back in our original places now. I want to hear someone propose a plan of some sort or for Troy to promise he will help at the very least.

Paul asks the sixty-four-thousand-dollar question as I hold my breath: "So, are you willing to help us?"

Troy is silent as if he's lost in thought. At last, he nods his head. "If I agree—but only if—it's on my terms. Do you understand?"

"What—you expect us to pay you or something?" Paul asks.

"No, I want full recognition if the experiment is successful. It will be noted, written up, recorded, and released to the public," Troy says in a finite tone. "I've had experiments fail in the past, but if this one is successful, I want to be known for it."

This man surely has some issues. He's not only rude but his ego is beyond comprehension. I realize I have to dismiss his attitude. I need him.

"I…don't see any problem with that, do you, Paul?" I ask, waiting patiently for Paul's reply.

Paul agrees. His next question is, "When do we start?"

Troy informs us that he needs to go over previous papers from the last time a volunteer went back, a few years prior.

Now, he has our attention. "What, exactly, happened to the last volunteer?" I have to ask.

Troy gives me a sharp look. His brown eyes seem to turn even darker, ones that have a hint of evil. "It didn't end well. We used my latest machine, the one I built with similar dimensions to that of scientist Morris Thorne's model, with a built-in particle accelerator, but it ran too hot and burned the volunteer pretty bad."

I put my hand over my mouth in horror. "Did he—"

"No, he's alive, but he suffered severe burns to his upper body," Troy confesses. "Look, I'm not here to injure people. I want this to be successful. I also want the notoriety that comes with it."

"I guess that means using the machine is out?" Paul asks.

"Yes. Without a doubt."

My patience is wearing thin. I ask, "How do you expect to accomplish this without a machine?"

"Your best bet is the portal method. The atmospheric conditions must be right, along with the alignment of the constellations at the time of travel. All work in divine synchronicity with the universe. The vibrations from the music you heard, along with the position of certain constellations in the sky, are what I believe propelled you here, and it will be a part of the plan that will propel you back."

It's all beginning to make sense now. At least, that's what my mind is telling me.

Troy tells me to go on my date with Dylan but pay attention to any signs or indications of things that might seem strange and report back to Paul the next day. In the meantime, he will go back over the research on time portals.

"Will we be traveling to Stonehenge or the Grand Canyon by any chance?" I ask only partially in jest.

Troy shakes his head. "Don't need to go that far. There are a few powerful places not far from here."

I sigh. My concerns about the effects of this type of journey fill my head. I turn to Troy. "What are the possible side effects of this kind of travel?"

"It's different for each individual. I can, however, tell that the common ones are the possibility of not returning to your desired location, ending up in the future or somewhere back in the past, or worst of all, getting stuck in a time warp and being lost to the ether."

In a casual tone, Troy explains that once I have reported back to Paul after my date with Dylan, Paul will contact him, and we will meet back here next weekend to discuss our plan.

"Not to worry," he says, "this isn't my first rodeo."

I sit here trying to digest all he's said. Once again, I can't believe the man's huge ego. I'm holding myself back fighting some choice words I'd like to say but dare to. I'm left with visions of myself free-floating through space. I think I'd rather ride a wild bull in a rodeo than what he's got planned. I can't help but wonder how many of his test subjects suffered some of the ill effects he mentioned.

I feel a panic attack set in, but Paul gives me a gentle pat on the back, and I feel a bit better, knowing we are ready to head outside to get some well-needed fresh air.

Troy escorts us to the front door with his henchman in tow. He reminds me not to pack. I don't appreciate his humor, but at least I still have some time to spend with my family and best friend.

# Chapter 31

The rest of the week seems to fly by in a flash, and Friday comes all too soon. I'm running on borrowed time here. I have a date with Dylan tomorrow, and on Sunday night, I have plans to go to Kent with Tracey and do our usual pub crawl. I shake my head, wondering how in the world I'm going to pull all of this off. Paul has been pressuring me to try to get more information out of Dylan. So far, he's pretty much clueless about everything I've told him…*or is he just playing me?*

Tracey calls to ask me what I plan to wear for my date on Saturday. She tells me she'll drive up to Kent on Sunday, knowing that I don't like driving home in the dark—I never have. She talks, but I can't seem to focus on her words. All I can think about is meeting Mark at McCarty's Irish Pub that Sunday night, the night that changed my life forever.

After we end our call, I need to head to Lanterman's Mill to clear my head and hopefully feel some vibes that might give me more answers. Lord knows I need them. My mind keeps playing with the thought that Troy or another member of the cult had put a spell on Dylan back in 2023, one that would enable him to transport both of us. Until I know otherwise, everyone is a suspect.

With that thought, I know I care for him—the Dylan from my past—but I fell in love with Mark, and I'm still in love with him. I'm going to see this journey through, come Hell or high water. I can only pray I don't wind up in the former.

It's late in the afternoon, and there are only a handful of people at the mill. I park my car and head for the building, carrying a small blanket under my arm. I pass by the gift shop, quicken my step, and find a cozy spot by the creek in the back. I plop down and take in the sweet smell of the large oak and maple trees. The air has a chill to it, but it's crisp and clean and smells like fall. I breathe deeply, watching the auburn leaves do their dance in the light breeze that's picked up.

It's not long before I feel drowsy again, so I close my eyes and lie down.

I hear Brandy calling my name as she wanders through a dense forest. She's walking in the rain and trudging along through the mud. She looks frail. Lost.

I'm awakened by voices. When I sit up, I see a small group of people walking by.

I must have been dreaming. I can't help but worry about Brandy. She must be looking for me. I tremble, knowing I may never see her again. I know I have to trust Troy and Paul—I have no choice. Paul seems more genuine than Troy. I can't put my finger on it, but there's something sinister about Troy. I hate that I might end up playing a role in his dark agenda to promote his own fame and glory.

The water rushing in the creek heralds my attention. I listen as if it's talking directly to me. "What's the message?" I ask, hoping some magical voice will answer, but there's nothing.

I wait and glance at my watch, noting the time. It's late, and I need to get going.

Thoughts of sitting down with my family for dinner tonight ground me. I need that. Everything around me lately is riddled with strangeness.

Mom's meatloaf is a welcome treat. Joe is gone again, but I am thankful I get to spend more time with Mom and Dad.

Dad asks me how I spent the afternoon, and I tell him where I went. He tells me that as a child, he used to spend hours at the mill with his older brother. "Nature is good for the soul," he says. His words surprise me. They're most unusual for him. I don't remember him ever imparting such words of wisdom as a child. *Since when did he become a sage?* I hold his gaze, wondering if, somehow, he knows what's going on.

*Nah! Can't be*, I reason.

It's good to climb into bed. I'd forgotten how comfy my old mattress was. It's a safe place.

I wake to see the sunlight peeking through my ruffled pink curtains. I've slept in until nine, which is so unlike me.

I pull on my robe and saunter downstairs. Mom and Dad have already had breakfast. They've been up since seven.

Mom pours me a cup of coffee and makes me some toast. She tells me the temperature will be going down to the fifties tonight, so I'd better take a jacket.

After breakfast, I make no haste before heading back upstairs and rummaging through my closet for something to wear to the party tonight.

*It's slim pickings in here.*

I figure I still have time to head to the local mall to pick up a new outfit, something sexy for Dylan, who said he wanted to show me off.

I don't need anything new for Sunday night—I'll wear the usual: some jeans and a short T-shirt. I run my hands over my youthful, flat stomach. How I wish I'd maintained my slim figure in my later years.

I ask Mom if she wants to come with me, but she declines, stating that it's her usual cleaning day. I know that. I promise her I won't be long, and I'll help her when I get back.

Dad hands me a fifty and tells me to have fun. I kiss him on the cheek. Yes, people still use cash, and fifty is enough to buy a decent dress.

Step Into Style is my first stop—it was one of my favorites back in the day. I head over to where the short party dresses are and pull three off the rack to try on. I get lucky—the third one I try on is the ticket. It's a black satin mini dress with spaghetti straps, and it fits perfectly. It's got a side slit, and I know how much Dylan likes my legs.

He calls shortly after I arrive home to remind me he'll be picking me up at seven. I tell him I have something special for him, and he asks if it is some lacey lingerie. I chuckle and tell him he'll just have to wait to see. I know he has sex on his mind, and so do I.

As I dress, I feel as if I'm getting ready for the prom. My heart races when I hold the satin mini dress up against my lean body and look at myself in the mirror.

I rummage through my undie drawer, searching for my black lacey bra and panties, knowing Dylan would want to see them. I want to please him, but I also want to gain information. Maybe this is the way to go: sex and then a confession—it's a good plan.

Listening to some of Velvet Thunder's songs gets me in the mood for the party tonight. I think about how Tracey would have loved to have been invited. At least she'll get all the sordid details from me on our drive up to Kent on Sunday.

Time is running out. I have at least half an hour before Dylan arrives. I pull my hair into a high ponytail, secure it with a black velvet ribbon, and add some rhinestone dangling earrings for some sparkle. I think about Troy and Paul's suggestion to pump him for details, surprised they don't have me wear a wire.

Dylan gives me the once over when I open the front door. "You look hot, babe!"

"You don't look so bad yourself," I say, eyeing his tight jeans and black wool blazer.

I grab my short gray jacket.

Mom yells from upstairs to have a good time, but Dad doesn't make an appearance.

Soon, we're zooming down US 224 toward Boardman on our way to the party. Dylan turns to me and says, "Just to let you know: there will most likely be drugs, booze, and other wild games going on tonight," not without a bit of concern.

I tell him not to worry. It's to be expected. He gives me a wink and places his hand on my thigh, sliding it up and under my dress. As if I didn't know he would. I remember these dates with him. I never partook in any of the sexual antics or drugs at these parties. The most

I'd ever done was a few tokes on a doobie. I wish I could say the same for Dylan.

He drives faster as his hand moves higher on my thigh and reaches my panties. "Mmm, I like what I see." He takes his eyes off the road, and we swerve, almost missing a truck. "See what you do to me, babe?"

"Well, if you want to see more of these things, we'd better make it there alive," I tell him.

We pull up to an impressive stone manor. I should have expected the house to be huge—*why shouldn't a famous band member own a mansion?*

We drive up into the circular driveway where the valet waits for us to exit the car.

Dylan takes my hand, and we walk through the large, wooden double doors. The music is blasting, and people are spread about the interior of the home, dancing. It's hard to hear anyone. My eyes are fixed on the beautiful spiral staircase and the people on it as they move up to the balcony to bust some wild moves.

Evan Marone, the band's lead singer makes his way through the crowd to greet us. His long black hair hangs past his shoulders and splays out over his red satin shirt. He knows Dylan, but he waits for him to introduce me.

"This is my date, Jennifer Kovich," Dylan says proudly, his arm tightly around me.

"I have to say that Dylan has great taste, my lady," Evan says, dutifully undressing me with his eyes. He tells us to make ourselves at home and escorts us into a room with a full bar. The party room is bigger than my entire house. There are two bartenders behind the counter, and Dylan asks me what I'd like to drink.

I order my usual rum and Coke while he orders his usual White Russian.

We carry our drinks around with us while Dylan eyes the activity in the den. Couples are making out on the large leather sofa, and there are some lying on the black high-pile shag rugs. One couple motions for us to come to join them, but Dylan waves his hand as if to gesture that we have no interest, and we make our way over to the kitchen area, where the caterers are preparing large silver trays of appetizers. I'm starving, so I grab a Swedish meatball on a stick and waste no time popping it into my mouth.

We make our way out onto the large screened-in patio in the back. It's chilly, but Dylan sees the drummer out there, and he wants me to meet him. He's sitting on a wicker-style couch with a young blonde girl, who looks as if she's under eighteen. They're both snorting Coke and are high as kites. Dylan introduces me to the stocky, dark-haired drummer, who rises from the sofa to give me a kiss on the cheek. I breathe a sigh of relief that it doesn't go any further. His date remains seated, most likely too stoned to move.

Evan wastes no time in offering us a sample of his best stash. He whispers something in Dylan's ear, which has me a bit unnerved.

Dylan takes my hand and leads me up the beautiful oak winding staircase. I ask him where we are going, and he tells me there are seven bedrooms here, and we're going to take the grand tour.

We pass by three rooms. He tries the doors but finds them all locked. I assume they are all occupied. We cross the hall, find one door open, and my eyes take in the beauty of this fine bedroom, decorated in white, gray, and black. The bed is round and has a white fur comforter. Tall, statuesque lamps of Greek goddesses sit on either side of it. A large, sliding glass door framed in black satin drapes leads to a small balcony. I turn and look up at the ceiling, expecting to see a mirror, but only see fine crown molding there. *Definitely masculine, but still sexy. I'm sure this dude hired an interior decorator.*

After a few hits of weed, I'm ready for a romp with Dylan. We stand by the bed making out, his tongue diving deep into my mouth. His hands slide my dress gently off to the floor, and he takes the time to admire my black lingerie. "You did this for me, babe?" he whispers in my ear.

He throws me onto the fur bed. I like the way it feels on my skin. He undresses down to his black briefs and lies on top of me, planting little kisses along my neck down to my navel. I love the way his hardness feels against my lace panties. I love that I can do that to him.

My wet folds welcome his member as he enters me slowly and pulls out, only to enter me even deeper and with harder thrusts. I dig my nails into his hard ass and ride him like a wild bull.

We come together and lie on the bed. Feeling sated, he sighs and tells me it was the best sex we've had yet.

I realize the moment to hit him with my barrage of questions has come. He's high, satisfied, and relaxed, and so am I. I roll over and kiss him lightly on the forehead. "Hey, babe—did you ever go to one of those meetings at that club Gregg wanted you to attend?"

"Just once. I think I told you. It's not my thing, but Gregg kept bugging me to go."

"I know you like astrology," I say, hoping to dig deeper.

"I do, but that club went into more things than I care to talk about."

*Hmm, maybe he's telling the truth. Either that or he's a damn good liar.*

"Do you remember me telling you all that stuff about how I got here?"

He looks at me quizzically. "Not that again. How much weed did you smoke?"

I huff and feel as if this is going nowhere. "I mean, do you ever feel a bit off when we're together?"

"The only thing that's going to be off is when I got off with you tonight."

I shake my head. *Ugh, really? This man!* I'm so frustrated at this point!

"I mean, do you ever feel as if you're caught in some sort of weird dream?"

"If this is a dream, I hope it never ends. I've fallen for you, hard."

I let the words settle, and they settle deep. I can't deny what I feel.

I see he's about to fall asleep on the bed, so I wait until he's passed out before heading back downstairs to see if Gregg is here. *Maybe he can fess up if he's high?*

The party has pretty much fizzled out, but the smell of pot still lingers. Most of the rooms are littered with leftover food and remnants of assorted drugs, and people are passed out everywhere. I walk into the large entertainment room to find Gregg slumped in an oversized chair, high as a kite. He's got some redhead sleeping next to him, wearing only a skimpy bra and panties. I try to rouse him but don't have much luck. *So much for getting information from him.*

I feel a hand on my shoulder and turn to find Evan Marone right behind me. "Hey, gorgeous—looks like your man took off."

"He…uh…he's asleep," I say, pushing his hand away.

"I've got some killer Angel Dust I'd love to share," he says in a tone that's deep and dark.

I decline and head back upstairs. I don't feel safe here. I want to go home. The whole place gives me the creeps. It's like some sort of zombie love fest. Who even knows if these people are real? The way things are going, I wouldn't be surprised if we were all caught up in some weird dimension.

# Chapter 32

It's good to be home. It's late, and I know everyone will be asleep except for Joe—his bike is gone. Dylan cuts the engine and turns to kiss me. "Good sex again, babe. I'll need a redo next weekend."

I stifle a sigh. *Will there even be a next weekend, seeing as how I have plans to meet with Troy and Paul this Wednesday about an attempt to travel back?*

I return his passionate kiss and tell him I'll call him in a few.

Dylan's abrupt peel-out forces me to turn around and watch him speed down the street. Watching him exit in his Camaro reminds me of the DeLorean in *Back to the Future*, where the car was the transport vehicle. I think about my Road Runner and wonder if, somehow, that could also be a means of transport for me. If so, then I hope Troy or Paul will say something. *Will they say something?*

I reek of stale weed and sex, and I'm eager to get undressed and take a shower. I walk softly past Mom and Dad's room, not wanting to wake them, and head for the basement to shower. I emerge, pull on my robe, and head upstairs to slip into bed. Tomorrow will be a big day. It's the day I'm going to meet Mark in Kent. I wonder how I'll deal with the situation. Once again, I pray to wake up in my own time so I can avoid all of this.

* * *

I awake to the scent of coffee, pull on my robe, and head downstairs. Mom and Dad are at the table, finishing up breakfast. They are dressed for church. Mom asks me if I'd like to go with her, but I tell her I'm tired from the party last night.

"You know, Jenn, I'm not forcing you to go to church, but it couldn't hurt once in a while," Mom says, carrying their mugs over to the sink.

Once her words sink in, I realize that maybe I do need to go to pray for all of this to stop. I've been keeping company with some questionable men lately, and who knows what might take place in the future.

"You're right, Mom. I'm going to make it a point to go next Sunday. I don't have plans to go out next weekend, so I won't be tired," I lie…again. I apologize for not keeping our date to Volant Mills and promise to make it up to her. She tells me not to worry, and that we have plenty of time.

I have to swallow hard on that one.

Dad pipes up, "By the way, how was the party?"

I tell him it was like any typical house party. He smiles and hugs me. "Just as long as you had a good time."

*Has he bought my story?* Once again, I have the feeling that he knows all too well what went on.

Tracey calls and I run upstairs to take her call from my room. I leave my freshly poured cup of coffee on the counter.

"You ready for tonight, girl?"

"I guess so."

"You guess so? What's up with you? Stay out too long last night? Too much sex?"

"It's not my type of scene. The party, I mean. I don't have to tell you what went on."

"Let me guess: orgies and drugs?"

"Pretty much."

She asks me what I plan to wear and tells me she'll pick me up at six, being that it will take us about fifty minutes to drive up to Kent. I remind her that Patti and Bev, our old high school girlfriends are meeting us there. She's not overjoyed, but she tells me the more the merrier. I vividly remember the light dose of resentment Tracey always had for Patti. She was always thinner and blonder than anyone else and always seemed to attract good-looking guys. Both girls were college grads now, and I always thought Tracey felt a bit inferior to them, but I don't know why because Tracey was and still is a knockout.

I lost touch with the girls a few years after I left Ohio back in 1977. They were both in my elementary education classes at YSU, and we enjoyed all of the frat parties on the weekends. It'll be good to see them again.

My stomach rumbles. I head back downstairs for some breakfast. I butter two pieces of toast and sit at the table, trying to recall what I wore the night I met Mark, but it's too far back.

*Damn time. It takes a real toll on the brain.*

I wash out my dish and cup in the sink and head up to my room to pick out an outfit. The Edge Bar was known to draw in quite an eclectic mix of people, not only with the local Kent crowd but also with people from other areas. Girls dressed sexy, though some opted for more hippie-like attire that's now popular in 2023. I pull out a pair of low-rise jeans and a glitter halter top. I must have had a real thing for halter tops, given that there were several in my drawers.

Having the afternoon to myself, I decide to go back over the notes on time travel in my notebook. Even though the guys have way more knowledge than I do on this sort of thing, I still want to be informed. Once again, I curse the fact I don't have access to the Internet here.

Mom and Dad have plans to drive over to my aunt Margie's house for the day and stay for dinner. They ask me to go, but I decline. She's always been one of my favorite aunts, but I can't bring myself to see her in the flesh—she passed away two years ago.

I tell Mom to hug her from me.

Joe still isn't home, and it's already four.

I have to step up my game and start getting dressed. I still have two hours, but it takes almost an hour to blow dry and straighten my hair, seeing as how I don't have a straightening iron here. I mean, who does?

Mom's ironed it out with an actual iron a few times, but it had dried out my hair.

Tonight is truly a special night. It's the night I'll meet Mark for the first time, that is in this time period. My pulse races with the mere thought of seeing him again.

I pull on my jeans and silver halter top, apply a heavy coat of silver eye shadow and black liner, and top it off with a few coats of pink lip gloss.

I grab my black pea coat and wait at the door for Tracey to pull up. I'm already feeling antsy, but I don't want to appear that way or give her any weird signals. She's already witnessed my odd behavior several times over.

"Wow, girl—you look hot," she roars as I slip into the passenger's seat. "You know, Dylan would be jealous if he saw you in that getup."

"Well, he's not going to be there, and I don't care if he'd be jealous. I'm free to dance with whomever I please tonight."

"Damn straight, girl, but promise me you won't get too wild and go home with some stranger."

I wink at her but don't make any promises.

* * *

There's minimal traffic on I76, and we make good time. The lot is already packed with cars when we arrive at the bar around 6:50. The marquee reads *Night Noise,* which explains the crowd. They are one of the best heavy metal bands out of Columbus.

Tracey parks in the back lot, and we walk toward the entrance, where two large, middle-aged men check out our IDs. We pay, and they stamp our hands with purple marks, the kind that lights up inside the dark club. The bar is teeming with young men and women, some with drinks in hand, the rest crowded around tall wooden tables. The stage area is set up with the band's instruments, and the dance floor is empty, but that will change soon.

We make our way through the crowd and over to a table close to the stage, wasting no time in claiming the table by throwing our jackets over the chairs.

Tracey's burgundy silk blouse catches my eye as it's in stark contrast with her dark blonde hair. I compliment her, and she blushes; I feel that was in order due to the fact that Patti would most likely arrive looking sexy as she always did. We order drinks, and I keep an eye out for the girls.

My attention is now drawn to the stage when a few of the band members enter, heading toward their instruments. They start warming up, and most of the chatter from the crowd halts.

A tall, thin guy with white leather pants and long brown hair picks up a guitar and speaks into the mic. "Hello, Kent! We are here to give you our best tonight!"

We all cheer and raise our glasses as the rest of the band takes the stage.

Tracey is quick to notice my fidgeting. "What's up with you, girl?"

"I guess I'm just anxious to dance. You know me."

"A little too well," she says as she moves her chair closer to mine. "Guess we have to make some room for Bev and Patti."

"Good plan." I have my eye on the door for them as well as three rough-looking hippie guys, who'll enter with their frontman, who looks like James Taylor (aka, Mark). That's one entrance I'll never forget.

I order another drink—I'll be needing it. Hell, I can even get sloppy drunk tonight, as I don't have to drive home.

I run to the restroom to check my makeup, and the first song begins to play. The music affects me, sending my adrenaline pumping. I return to the table, grab Tracey, and head for the dance floor. Others follow, and we're soon busting some moves.

After the third song, I'm already sweaty as we head back to the table to catch our breath.

I see Bev and Patti walk by the bar and wave them over. It's hard to miss Patti in her sexy, red, knit mini dress.

Tracey rolls her eyes.

Bev is more of the conservative type, wearing jeans and a green sweater.

We all hug and let out a shout when the band starts up their second set. Tracey's sitting this one out with Bev, so Patti and I take the floor. We must be a sight to see, as several guys have their eyes on us.

Why I'm startled when I see Mark walk toward the bar with his two mangy hippie friends in tow, I don't know. I watch him as he leans against the bar in that long green army coat, his long, shiny black hair hanging to his shoulders. It's clear his eyes are also on me. I feel dizzy and tell Patti that I need to sit for a bit.

Back at the table, Tracey notices my pallor and asks me if I'm all right.

I tell her I'm overheated and need some water, and she's quick to get me a glass. "No more drinks for you," she states.

Tracey, Bev, and Patti order a round of rum and Cokes. I guzzle my water and try to slow my breathing, but my heart keeps racing.

Some short guy with a blond shag haircut comes up to the table and asks Patti to dance. She takes a sip of her drink and lets the short guy lead her to the floor.

Tracey whispers in my ear, "See that guy over by the bar, the one in the long coat? He keeps looking at you. I think he likes you."

I nod. *I'd love to tell her that he's my future husband, but she'd start insisting that I see a shrink again.*

She pokes me in the arm, "Here he comes!"

Sure enough, my Mark pads his way toward my chair. "Would you like to dance?" he asks, pushing a few strands of his long bangs out of his eyes.

I freeze and feel as though I'm about to faint as I stare into his cool blue eyes.

"Something wrong?" he asks.

I get the strength and courage to stand. "Uh…no. I'm just catching my breath."

He takes my hand and leads me to the floor as the band is about to play the next song. It's a fast song, so I'm grateful, but it's one that Dylan's band also plays. We move to the music without much banter. A few tears roll down my cheeks. He's quick to notice and asks what it is. I tell him the song has a special meaning for me. He nods, and we move closer together.

He asks me my name, and he tells me his. He's quick to place his hand on the small of my back and lead me back to the table as the song ends.

All the girls are at the bar, so the table is empty.

Mark takes the seat next to mine and tells me that I'm so sexy. I blush and pray my eyes aren't too red from the tears. He edges his chair closer, asks me for my number, pulls a small piece of paper out of his coat pocket, and writes it down. I try to keep my humor about this archaic system under control as he folds the paper and tucks it back into his pocket.

"I'll call you soon," he says and kisses me on the cheek.

I watch him walk away. It's almost impossible to control my emotions this time. I'm out of control.

The girls walk back over to the table. Tracey is the first to boast. "I told you that guy had the hots for you—"

"What the hell's gotten into you now?" she says, obviously having noticed the streaks of mascara running down my cheeks.

I wipe my eyes with a cocktail napkin. "Dunno. Guess I'm just confused."

"Oh, I guess you're thinking about Dylan," Tracey surmises.

"Must be."

Tracey fills the girls in on my recent encounter with the hot rocker.

The band announces it's about to play its last set. Tracey pulls on my arm, and we head for the floor. I'm trying to put on my best front, but it's hard. My eyes are fixed on Mark as he walks off toward the front exit with his friends. I want to run after him and tell him everything, but I know it would be futile.

It's at that moment I realize who I am really in love with.

# Chapter 33

It's no surprise to get a phone call from Paul on Monday morning. He's anxious to hear if I have any dirt on Dylan to report, and much to our dismay, I have none. The only juicy news I can report is that the party was pretty much a gang-bang with everyone taking a lot of drugs, Dylan included. Of course, I don't mention that I'd met my future husband at a club last night. I'm not sure why I've held this information back, seeing as how I've already divulged just about everything to him. I reason it may be due to the fact it's irrelevant or too intimate. What I do tell him is that I need to go back as soon as possible and by any means.

He brings up a request for a music tape from the band, and I tell him I will get a copy this week. I can no longer hold back my curiosity and ask him exactly what it will be used for.

When he tells me, I'm surprised I haven't thought of it myself. He says that it was the enchanted music that brought me here, and it will be instrumental in my upcoming journey back home. He tells me he'll need it to bring it over to Troy at Orion's Path for an energy charge.

"What is that, exactly?" I ask, waiting for another piece of dark information.

"Troy has a special energy box he'll set the tape in to sort of infuse it and amplify its powers. I'll explain more when we meet with him."

"Is he going to electrocute it?"

"Not really. It's all a part of the science research he's done, but I like that you've still managed to have a sense of humor."

"My humor's short-lived, Paul."

Paul informs me of a quick meeting at Troy's on Thursday night. He tells me I should bring the tape with me.

As soon as we end the conversation, I get a call from the local school district. They need someone to substitute teach tomorrow for grade three. I stumble when I answer, having been caught off guard.

"I…I have a doctor's appointment, but please keep me on your active list."

Mom hears me on the upstairs phone and comes up to inquire who it is. I tell her about the job offer, and she tells me not to decline the next time as it could lead to a permanent offer. She hugs me, pulls back, and says, "Is everything okay? You seem a bit tense these days."

"I know. I'm still not sure about my relationship with Dylan." More lies.

She tells me what she always tells me, that I am young and I should never settle.

I give her another hug, and she informs me that she's leaving for work, but the coffee's still hot. I pad downstairs to pour myself a cup. Joe has left for work as well Dad. I decide to call Dylan to let him know that I need the tape before Thursday. I tell him I'm driving to Akron for a job interview and want to listen to his music on the way. *It amazes me how easily I come up with these lies.*

He agrees to meet me for lunch on Wednesday, and he'll hand off the tape then.

I head for my room but something instinctively guides me to go into Mom and Dad's instead. Mom always kept her St. Jude medal in a small crystal dish on her dresser. I pick it up and let it rest in my palm, feeling the energy it emits. It's good energy. Her energy. Far better than the type I believe Troy Duncan possesses.

I want to take it with me, but I remember reading stories about others who've time traveled not being able to take possessions with them. I wonder how accurate all of this information is as I set the medal back down in the small dish.

My stomach rumbles as I pull into Bunch of Lunch, and my head begins to pound as I know I need to be in a state of normalcy whenever I'm with Dylan.

He waves at me from a booth at the back near the restrooms and stands to hug me. I detect Paco Rabanne, his signature scent, on him.

His tight-fitting T-shirt accentuates his toned body beneath it and has me wanting to grab him right here.

*What the hell is with me? Does he possess some magic, as well, or did this time travel thing turn me into a slut?*

I let that thought go and slide into the black vinyl booth instead.

The waitress is quick to deliver our menus and two glasses of water.

"So, I brought the tape," he says as he slides it across the table.

"Thank you."

"I hope this will ease your drive to Akron."

I sigh, thinking about how easy this all was. I hate having to deceive so many people. It's not me, but I figure that this is my only chance to get any answers.

He asks me about the interview, and I struggle for words. "It's…it's a grade-four position. I wanted the earlier grades, but hey, at least it's a start."

"Damn straight. They'd be lucky to have you." He grabs my hand, and I just about melt.

We order two burgers and a side of fries to share. I slip the tape into my fringed suede shoulder bag and notice that his eyes are still on me. I am mesmerized as I look into those hazel eyes. *Damn, he always has the same effect on me. Why the hell am I so weak?*

"You're tense, Jenn—what's up?"

"Oh, it's this interview. I get so nervous about things like this."

"You got this, and you know it."

We are pretty much quiet during the rest of lunch. When we're done, he checks his watch, tells me he has a few hours to kill, and suggests we go back to his apartment.

I know he has sex on his mind, and I always give in to him, but this time, something in me strikes a different vibe, and I tell him I need to get home to finish filling out the paperwork for the interview.

He nods and tells me he understands and that he'll pick me up on Sunday night to accompany him to an outdoor concert at Midway Park.

"I'm looking forward to it," I say as I stand to kiss him.

He puts his hand on my ass and gives it a light pat. "Drive safe, and let me know when you get back." He remains in the booth and orders another beer.

I walk toward the door but stop to look back just before I'm about to leave, having realized that if all goes well, this may be the last time I see him. I wipe the tears from my eyes with the sleeve of my jacket and head out to the parking lot.

When I get home, I call Paul and tell him I have the tape. His voice reassures me that all will fall into place. He reminds me not to listen to it until Friday night, the night of my so-called travel.

No sooner do I hang up with Paul than I get a call from Mark. "I'm sorry to call you so soon, but I couldn't stop thinking about you," he says, his voice soft.

"Well, I have been thinking about you, too," I confess.

"Really? How about I take you to La Biasco's restaurant on Saturday night…that is if you like Italian food."

"Are you kidding me? I'm half Italian."

"I bet you're a good cook."

"No, but my mother is."

"Is 6 p.m. a good time for you?"

I take in a deep breath. *Who even knows if I'll still be here?*

"You still there?" he asks.

"Yes. I was just looking at my calendar. It's good. I can't wait to see you."

I sit on the edge of my bed, rubbing my temples. If I go successfully back Friday night, I'll miss the chance to see him and maybe relive our history together.

My head hurts. I reach for some Aspirin in the bathroom medicine cabinet and decide to take a short nap, but I keep tossing and turning with that tape in my line of vision on my dresser. My brain finally snaps to, and I realize I do have an eight-track player in my car. If that tape only knew the power it possessed.

# Chapter 34

I hardly slept last night, thinking about my meeting tonight with Troy and Paul. I wish I could tell Tracey, but I realize that's not at all possible. It's only ever been Paul, Troy, and me in on this, and it hasn't been easy. These thoughts bring me back to Tracey and I realize I have to call her today to see if I can pop over. I have to see her one more time.

I also have to ready myself to leave tomorrow evening, and I have three of the most important people in my life to bid goodbye to. If this experiment goes down the rabbit hole, I'll be lost somewhere in time; God only knows where.

With me alone in the house again, I have the time to analyze my situation more deeply, but the more I read over the research papers and notes, the more confused I become. Too bad science has yet to make the progress it has in 2023 I've read that the government perfected time travel and uses it for high-powered, secret operations, but I can't simply call them and ask for their help or to be another one of their guinea pigs. Then again, I don't trust them any more than I do Paul and Troy.

I get Tracey on the second ring. She's rushing off to work. I guess she detects the uneasiness in my voice because she asks me what's wrong.

I tell her I'm nervous about starting my subbing job. She supports me by saying how lucky they are to have me and asks me to go back up to Kent this coming weekend. There's silence on my end as my eyes begin to well up. It's good that my last goodbye will be via the phone. Now that I think of it, I'd fall apart if I saw her in person.

I accept her offer even though I realize I might not be here. I tell her I love her and thank her for being there for me when I needed her. We end the call, my eyes welling up again.

Mom is home now, and I'm delighted to help her start the tuna casserole. It was something I watched her make growing up that I continued to make well into my adult years.

"So, did the district office give you another call?" Mom asks, chopping an onion.

"No, but I'm confident something will come soon."

Dad comes in and mentions the fact that we are making his favorite meal. I turn to give him a big hug, and he holds on tightly as if he doesn't want to let go. Once again, I have to wonder if he has some insight into everything that's been happening. *Nah, couldn't be, could it?*

* * *

I try to steady my hands as I pick out something to wear from my closet. The October evenings have gotten colder, so I opt for a button-down red sweater and comfy jeans. I take it that the meeting at Orion's Path will be an informative one, so there's no use in breaking out the party clothes. Besides, Paul said there were no services for members tonight, and it would just be the three of us. This has me feeling even more uneasy.

My drive over to Orion's Path seems to take longer than usual. I'm not sure why. Few cars are on the road, and my attention is drawn to the majestic oaks and maple trees Nature has painted vibrant hues of gold and burgundy. How I've missed this. I slow down to take it all in. It's as if they want me to admire their beauty, knowing it is fleeting. I accept their invitation, not knowing what lies ahead of me, and turn into the long gravel driveway leading up to the cabin.

I park in the back lot next to Paul's shiny MG. I figured he'd get here early, wanting to set up things with Troy before I arrive. I grab my wool jacket, slip the cassette tape into my bag, and head for the back door.

Paul greets me at the door, minus the henchman. He's also in jeans and has on a green blazer that brings out the green in his hazel eyes, the ones I look into and feel a bit of uneasiness.

"What's up?" I whisper.

"Nothing. I just want everything to go as planned. Troy and I were discussing the Morris-Thorne Wormhole Theory versus Kozyrev's Time Wave Method, and we seem to disagree a bit."

"Well, I'd be the last person to give my opinion. I'm depending on both of you to make this happen," I say as I pull out the tape from my bag.

Paul's eyes light up like a kid on Christmas morning. "Ah! We have our most important instrument here. You haven't listened to it, have you?"

"Of course not. I followed your instructions."

Paul slips the tape into a pocket in his blazer, and I follow him down to the basement, where I assume Troy is already at work. We walk through a sitting area that could pass for someone's living room, with its paneled walls and shag carpet, and enter another door that leads to the secret lab. I get goosebumps and feel the atmosphere change once in the lab with all of the strange electrical equipment and chemicals burning in different colored beakers. It resembles one of those dark ones I've seen in science fiction movies.

Troy turns away from the old workbench to greet me. "Here's the lady of the hour," he says, and I detect a bit of a naughty gleam in his eye. The way he's dressed reminds me of a mad scientist. He's wearing a long green apron over his clothes and removes his leather glove to shake my hand. Troy tells us to have a seat on the wooden bench to the side of the counter, where more beakers are displayed. "I need to finish calibrating this makeshift accelerator to get the micro-black hole to work. I'm sure Paul has filled you in on the wormhole method we are going to use."

I turn to Paul with a quizzical look. Paul winks at me.

We watch Troy enter a small back closet, bring out a large, square metal box, and set it up on the main work table. He tells Paul he will let him know when to bring up the tape.

I feel as though we're both at Troy's mercy. Though I used to think he and Paul were in this together, now I feel as if Troy has completely taken over.

We watch Troy as he adjusts some thick wires and connects them to the box. "Once we inflate the particle accelerator and infuse it with negative mass, it's going to be hot and ready to use. Let me finish this, and I'll go over a few changes for tomorrow night."

"Changes?" I look to Paul.

"Not to worry. It's all under control," he whispers into my ear.

"Will Orion's Belt provide the wormhole tomorrow night?" Paul asks.

Troy is too preoccupied to answer Paul's question. But I know he's purposely ignoring him.

Paul stands and walks over to Troy. "You know that wormholes are unstable and constantly moving."

"I'm aware. I have everything under control. Trust me, this isn't my first rodeo." He pulls on a newer set of black gloves. "Now, hand me the tape," he commands.

I don't like the way Troy orders Paul around. My eyes are fixed on Paul as he stands there, watching Troy fiddle with more cables. I can even sense the agitation coming from Paul.

Troy instructs me to come over to the workbench. "I've been working diligently on the process and have decided that I will be accompanying you tomorrow night to make sure it all works properly. I can't let any of the equipment malfunction."

"Do you mean to say that you'll be traveling to my time as well? Y-you'll be with me?" I feel my eyes starting to bulge from shock.

"Yes, because I'm not sure what will happen, but this is all a part of science. I want to be the one who makes this successful. I've worked too hard to let this fail, and I can't let you alone with this system and fuck it all up."

His words hit me hard. The pressure in my head is unbearable. I feel dizzy. The room begins to spin, and I have to sit down. I hear

Troy's voice demanding that Paul hand over the tape again, and I put my head between my knees for fear I am about to black out.

The sound of a gunshot pulls me out of my state. I jump up to see Troy lying on the floor in a pool of blood spilling from his forehead onto the cracked concrete floor.

Paul has a gun in his hand. It appears to be a Colt Python. I recognize it because Joe has one just like it.

I scream, kneeling on the floor, feeling faint again.

Paul slips the gun back into his blazer, comes over, grabs my arm, and leads me out of the room, up the stairs, and off the compound. I feel as though I'm in another dream and a bad one at that. Paul tells me to give him my keys and get into my car, and everything will be all right. I do exactly as he says. I don't have any other choice.

I close the door and turn to Paul. "What the hell? You killed him?"

"I had to, Jenn. It was the only way. His plan was not foolproof. It was dangerous, and you most likely would have been killed. His only goal was to use you and the experiment for his own gain."

"How do you know all of that?"

Paul starts the engine and peels out of the driveway. "We need to get out of here. I'll tell you as soon as we're on the highway."

It's not long before we're on the on-ramp. Paul takes a moment to merge into traffic, and then he says, "When I arrived early, he told me the new plan, but he didn't mention the fact that you might not have survived the journey, not with his method, anyway. You most likely would have been burned to a crisp just like all the others, but he had the means to survive. He planned to divert the high-powered beams from the energy box to your side of the car, which would have emitted too strong of a beam. One connection from the box needed to be stronger to equalize both outlets. He knew exactly what he was doing. I played along with him until you arrived, but I wasn't about to let you go into this blind, or killed!"

I sit here in a daze, not believing what I'm hearing. *Where are my comforting trees now?*

"But you murdered him," I manage to say. "You'll go to jail!"

"No, I won't. I will dispose of the body. As soon as I drop you off, I'm coming back to clean it up and bury his body out in the woods. He had a lot of enemies, not to mention there's a radical Christian group rumored that wants to take him out. They will get the blame. Then again, no body, no crime. Some might even believe he went off to conduct some weird experiment."

"How are you going to get back there? I mean, your car's in the lot."

"Not to worry. I'm walking up to DeFranco's Market where there's a ride waiting for me. I also need to go back to the compound, retrieve the tape, and recalibrate it. You'll need it."

I shake my head. "I don't know, Paul. I mean—"

"Listen to me: you are still going home tomorrow night. I have a plan. I've always had a backup plan. Trust me."

I'm still in shock, but I listen as he drives, wondering who this other person is who would take him back to the compound.

Then I realize that I was there when it happened—*would I be implicated in the murder? What if someone saw us?* Then again, I realize the cops won't be able to find me if I'm back in 2023.

I listen as Paul goes over the final details: "The plan is for you to sit in your car in the Regal Room parking lot tomorrow night just before midnight when Orion's Belt is at its brightest. You will listen to the tape after it's been energized in the accelerator. There will be no energy box in your car, but I will place three concave mirrors in the car, one in the front and one on each side. You will touch each one so it makes contact with your energy. This will create a Time Waver that will help the stars, the time, and the pattern of events that brought you here to communicate. It's a method by Russian scientist Nikolai Kozyrev that I've studied. The mirrors act as semiconductors, allowing the music's vibrations to bounce off of them. You will be at your point of entry and be safely transported by the energy from the mirrors on your way back home. If you want to go, you need to go tomorrow because I need to leave."

"Where will you go?"

"My grandmother's in upstate New York. She's already waiting for me. I will wait until you're all set to go, but then I need to take off."

I'm still shaking when Paul pulls into my driveway. He holds me tightly, telling me all will be okay. "How can it ever be okay when you did this for me?" I whimper.

"Not only did I do it for you, Jenn, but for everyone who might fall prey to Troy's sinister methods so he could make a name for himself in the science world."

I pull back, letting it all sink in, his words trying to ease my *mea culpa,* but they don't even come close. "I'm worried, Paul. I've changed history while I've been here. What will that do to my future in 2023?"

"No matter what you do, salient events will calibrate around you. These events always adjust themselves to avoid inconsistencies. I've learned that from my studies of Germain Tobar, an honors student in the field of science from Australia.

"Unbelievable." I take in a long breath. "He sounds just like another you."

"Don't know if that's a good or bad thing, Jenn."

"You won't hear from me until we meet in the back parking lot tomorrow night at 11:30. I suppose you'd better say your final goodbyes, 'cuz you sail at midnight tomorrow."

# Chapter 35

I had hoped all of this was just another bad dream, but I wake up in the same bedroom. My mind tries to process what happened last night. There was a murder, and now I'm down to only one man who might be able to get me back to my time, but not if he gets arrested first. I've never witnessed a murder before, and I'm still shaken to the core. Now, I have no other choice than to trust Paul with my life. *Was he right about Troy? Is my life in danger if I proceed with his plan? Who knows?* All I do know is that I'm desperate to get back home.

The new plan does not have me returning to Lanterman's Mill. I hoped it would be my transport, as I feel connected to that place. Then again, what did I know about any of this?

Remembering Paul's words from last night hits me hard. I wonder whether to call Mark and Dylan and cancel my upcoming dates, but I might still be here. I'm going to say my final goodbyes to my family, but not in a way that would alarm them or lead them to believe I'm losing my mind. There's no way I'll ever let them onto the fact I might be gone.

*Then again, will I be gone? If this is the past, shouldn't I still be here, carrying on with my life in this realm?* My head hurts from too much thinking. I need caffeine, and I need it now.

I catch Mom before she goes to work. Joe's up early as well, getting ready for a biker outing with some of his buddies. I catch him just as he's packing his gear in the Harley's side saddlebag.

"Hey, I want to tell you to drive safe but enjoy yourself. I hoped you'd be here for our usual Friday night fish fry tonight at the Fish Station. You know it's a family tradition."

"Yeah, me, too, but it's almost a five-hour drive to Arlington, Va. Wanna get a head start to check into the hotel before the events start."

"I know you enjoy your biker conventions or whatever you call them, so have a great time and go easy on the beer." I hug him and don't want to let go. I think about his ability to repair bikes and how it will lead to a great job as an airline mechanic in the future, but he doesn't know that now.

He flashes me a huge grin and his bushy mustache wiggles. "You got it, Sis."

I stand in the driveway, watching with Mom as he takes off. Mom turns to me, her silver hair done in a perfect flip. "I take it you'll be home tonight to join me and Dad for fish dinner?"

"I wouldn't miss it for the world."

* * *

Tracey gives me a quick call before work. "Just checking up on you. I sensed something was bothering you when we spoke last time."

"It's nothing. It's just that this Mark guy has asked me out, and I don't know how to deal with Dylan."

"Why not play the field?"

I ponder my response before saying, "I hear you, but these things never end well."

She asks me if I'm still on for Friday night at the Regal Room, and my body just about freezes over. "You still there?"

"Yeah, I'm here. Yes, I'd love to go," I say, knowing I'll be there but sitting in the parking lot, waiting for my Road Runner to transport me back home. I'm not about to go into it now, seeing as it's always been a no-win situation.

We end our call, and I think about my car sitting in the Regal Room's lot while the band plays inside to a packed club, its patrons unaware of the supernatural event taking place just outside. *Maybe it'd be better if I had a DeLorean for the trip after all?*

I head to my room to get my thoughts in order. I keep waiting for the phone to ring, hoping it will be Mark. The phone does ring but when I answer it, Dylan's on the other end. "Hey, babe!"

He tells me there's been a change in plans, and his band has been called to play at The Regal Room tonight as the other band's lead singer is ill. "I want you to be there," he says.

I take a deep breath, and the hairs on the back of my neck stand up. "I…I already promised some friends I'd meet them at that new club in Boardman. The Basement? I'm sure you've heard of it."

"Yes, but I'll miss my favorite dancer, making me hornier than ever."

*Stop! Stop*! My head pounds. *Why? Why does he do this?*

"Sorry, Dylan. Maybe we can all get together later," I say in an attempt to appease him.

"Sounds good. I'll save the best song for when I see you."

*Oh, I'm sure he will. I want to hate him, but I don't. If someone has put a spell on him, then maybe it's been cast on me, as well.*

My thoughts turn to Paul. *I pray that everything went down smoothly last night. Then again, how could everything have gone smoothly when there's a body that needs hiding?*

*Dear God!*

A wave of guilt washes over me. *It's all my fault. If I didn't need to make the journey back, Paul never would have gotten into this mess. And Dylan was quite possibly the one who'd gotten us all into this mess. Then again, Paul seemed to have taken on this task with great passion, making me wonder.*

The smell of everything fried hits me as I walk into the Fish Station with Mom and Dad. Mom walks as fast as lightning to get to her favorite booth close to the bar. The restaurant is dimly lit by small ceramic lamps gracing the center of each table. The bar is crowded with people, most of them fresh off work and ordering rounds of beer. I sit across from Mom and Dad as Betty, our usual waitress, brings us three menus. Betty knows Mom, and they exchange pleasantries before Betty comments on how she likes the green Angora sweater I'm wearing. It was a special birthday gift from last year. I reflect on how I always had the best growing up.

Dad takes a sip of his water and grabs my hand. "Any plans for tonight?"

"Actually, I do."

"You and Tracey going to the Regal Room?"

He catches me off guard, and I search for the words. "I…I'm meeting with some new friends from Kent, and we're going over to a new club in Boardman."

"It's good to expand your circle and make new friends, Jenn. You will meet new people throughout your life, some good, some bad, but you will encounter both."

I smile and think about all the advice he's given me over the years. I've never forgotten any of it. I stare into his cool blue eyes. "And I'm looking forward to it." *If he only knew I had recently met a few of those bad ones, and really bad ones, at that.*

We stuff ourselves with the delicious fried cod, fries, and coleslaw as we always do. Mom tells us we have some leftover cake at home, but I tell her I can't eat another bite. "I think they may need to roll me outta here," I say, patting my stomach.

Dad laughs.

I check my watch, knowing I have a few hours left to prepare and only a few hours left in this realm. I enter my bedroom and look around as if it were an old friend with whom I'll soon need to part ways, and I open a few drawers to look for some of my favorite items. I hold a silky blue nightgown up to my face, letting the scent of my body lotion permeate my nostrils. I look through the collection of albums in my stereo cabinet. I shake my head. *We had some damn good music at the time.*

I think of Dylan's band. They have plans for a gig in LA next year. He says they're going to make it big, but I know better—they'll never be more than a popular local band.

I sigh, thinking about the guy possibly responsible for bringing me here. *He and his magic, or whatever the hell he used. It had to be the only logical explanation for this phenomenon.*

I head back to my closet to select the proper outfit for my journey. Something comfortable will do the job. I mean, who knows if I'll be tumbling down some wormhole tunnel or flying through the clouds? I decide on jeans, a Pink Floyd T-shirt, and my short navy wool jacket.

Mom and Dad are in their room with the TV on. It's their usual evening routine. I pad in softly. All is dark except for the light from the TV. I walk over and kiss each of them. I'm holding back, and it's killing me. I tell them I won't be out all night, that the people I'll be with are good people, and not to worry.

No sooner am I out in the hall than I lose it, sobbing as I head down the stairs to grab my keys and make my way to meet Paul.

It's now or never. There's no turning back now.

# Chapter 36

The twenty-minute drive up to The Regal Room seems like an hour. I don't even look at my speed, but I know I'm crawling as I head for my so-called transport area. Now, with Dylan's band in there playing, it puts a whole new spin on everything. *Will I regret this?* If the experiment fails, I may be propelled into some unknown era, disfigured, aged, or even lost in some wormhole, but Paul has reassured me his method is safer as it uses a connection to Orion's Belt and lets the universe steer the wheel, so to speak. *I guess one can always trust the universe*, I reason.

I see the front parking lot is full when I pull in at exactly 11:30, drive through, and make my way to the far back parking lot, hoping no one will see my car. I was a regular here, and a lot of people know me and my car. I pray no one interrupts my plans.

Paul is leaning up against his car door. He has a black satchel with him. I park next to him, cut the engine, and leave my jacket in the car as it's an unusually warm night for October.

"Hey," I say. As I greet him, I notice his attire. He has on a black leather jacket and tight jeans, looking like some kind of secret agent. I'm surprised he isn't wearing dark sunglasses.

"You ready, Jenn?" he asks, tilting his head and then brushing his long, jet-black bangs out of his eyes with his hand. He looks me up and down. "You didn't bring any of your personal belongings with you?"

"No. All I have are the clothes on my back and my watch.

"I don't know if I'm ready, but let's do this."

"Just to let you know, that's Dylan's band playing in there. They are filling in for some other band tonight."

"Look, the clock is ticking. I've got to get into your car, set up the concave mirrors, and give you the tape. And I didn't know about the band. Now, give me your watch." His tone is quite demanding.

"Will this affect my journey?"

"What, the watch?" He looks at me quizzically.

"I mean the fact that Dylan's in there tonight."

"Shouldn't. Not if you stay strong. Keep focused on where you want to be. No matter what feeling comes over you to pull you away from this, push them off. It's imperative."

Paul must read my heavy breathing as a build-up of nerves. "Look up in the sky," he says, trying to get me to focus. "See over there—Orion's Belt?" He points to the brilliant constellation.

I look up, and it is as brilliant as ever. I can't take my eyes off of it, having never seen it so bright before. It's quite mesmerizing. I've never really paid much attention to this type of thing before.

Paul instructs me to get into his car while he sets up the mirrors in the Road Runner. He puts on a pair of white gloves and tells me he'll set the tape on the passenger's seat.

"Is it safe to touch? I mean, it was super-charged."

"Yes, it's safe. Now, we need to hurry. This has to be done by midnight."

I watch as Paul affixes the three small mirrors inside the car. Two are on the sides, and one is right on the front windshield, facing the driver's side. I shake my head. I can only imagine what might happen if anyone sees us. What if the security guard comes out?

My pulse races, and I'm sweating like crazy.

Paul comes back to the car and sits inside with me. "It's all set, Jenn. It's show time, girl!"

I hug him, and he holds me tightly. "It's going to be all right. Now, safe travels. You have a few people waiting for you back in 2023."

He slips out of the passenger's seat and closes the door. I watch him pull away and feel as though I've been deserted now that I'm on my own.

I can hear the band playing from here. I roll down my window, wanting to hear them one more time. Dylan is right up on that stage right now, playing and singing. My body shakes at the mere thought of it. I want to run inside and see him one more time, but then I remember Paul's words: "Be strong, Jenn. Be strong."

There is silence now. No music comes from the building. I look at the tape on the passenger's seat, start the engine, insert the eight-track into the player, and the music starts to play. I switch buttons over to the last track to hear the song "Dark Wicked Woman," and it's as if heat waves are pulsing throughout my body. My heart begins to race. The words sink deep into the recesses of my brain.

That's when the mirrors begin to spark. I sit back in my seat, afraid of being shocked. A beam of light comes through the front windshield and bounces off both of the side mirrors. The music seems to fade a bit, and the light beams bounce back and forth from mirror to mirror. Then one hits my chest, and I feel lightheaded. I try to bend forward to put my head between my knees, but space is tight in the front seat.

A familiar voice calls my name. It's faint, but I recognize it: it's Dylan's.

He's in the parking lot, heading toward the car. "Jenn! Don't go!"

I block out his words by covering my ears. I don't want to see him. "No! Go away!"

I'm too dizzy to sit up straight. I have to lean back in the seat.

My car spins so fast now that I have no control.

Everything goes black.

# Chapter 37



*Jennifer 2023*

My eyes flutter open as though heavy curtains are being drawn apart. Groggy and disoriented, I make an effort to blink away the sleep that clings to my vision. The softness beneath me feels foreign, unlike the leather seat of my car. I raise a hand to touch the fabric, confirming its reality. It's my only link to the past, a reminder of where I am.

My comfy sofa, the familiar wooden accents, and the pictures on the table—they all tell a story I know by heart. It's my family, my haven.

I ease myself into a sitting position, trying to get my bearings. A turquoise ginger jar lamp casts a warm glow over the room, illuminating memories that have been momentarily clouded.

The wall clock's bold digits declare it's three a.m., a stark reminder that time has a way of bending, distorting, and conforming to its own rules. My heart pounds and my thoughts and emotions are in a whirlwind. So many questions bubble up in my brain: *How? Why? What happened?*

I sweep my hands over my body, making a curious inventory of limbs and senses. Relief washes over me: all accounted for, but the fabric against my skin, a soft pink robe, is a poignant reminder of a transformation that defies every notion of logic I've ever known.

The bathroom mirror beckons like a portal of revelations. With trepidation and urgency, I cross the room to face myself, to confront the reflection of my past in my present. My hand trembles as it brushes against the cool glass and my breath catches in my throat as a familiar face gazes back, lines etched across it. It's my face, bearing the scars of life's battles and victories. The traces of gray woven into my hair from the roots are a testament to the passage of time and the wisdom strands acquired over the years.

I close my eyes, letting the weight of my thoughts settle, and a cascade of emotions crashes over me.

Paul.

His name reverberates through my consciousness like a mantra, and the doubt that once clung to my vision now dissipates like the morning mist. Paul, the enigmatic young science student who dared to bend time as he crafted a path for me.

For us.

A smile tugs at the corners of my lips as gratitude floods my heart. He believed when I couldn't. He saw what I couldn't. It was his genius that bridged the chasm between the past and the present, between disbelief and reality. Still, I can't stop a thought from invading my brain, and it's a dark one: the murder that happened that night.

I quickly push it out of my mind, knowing it was done in self-defense. It was Paul's only way to take care of what he needed to accomplish for both of us.

The concept of time remains an elusive dance of reality. My weeks away were but mere hours here, a fact that baffles me.

I wander back to the living room, my steps light yet laden with the weight of this knowledge. The CD that was my lifeline to the past rests in my hand. Last I remember, it was an eight-track cassette. It's a reminder of my journey, a testament to the unknown forces that guided me.

With a determined stride, I venture out to the garage to find my tool kit for a hammer. It's likely the only thing able to obliterate this connection that transcends time.

The plastic shatters and a sense of closure washes over me, cleansing my spirit of doubt and uncertainties.

My body is fighting signals that rest is needed, but how can I sleep? My mind races like a carousel of revelations. Tomorrow, the world will demand its dues, the threads of explanations woven into my new reality, *but who would believe me? A few didn't believe me back in '76—who would buy my story now?*

The memory of Dylan's voice, a lifeline through the abyss, echoes in my ears as my consciousness wanes, but the enigma persists: *was any of it real? Was it truly a rift in time's fabric, a glitch that defies understanding?*

A distant bark from the neighbor's dog rouses me from my sleep. Guess I did manage to succumb to a few hours of slumber. I emerge from dreams that are a tapestry of memories woven together with threads of uncertainty. The comforter slides back as my feet touch the floor, connecting with the present yet still somehow tethered to the past. The clock reads 7 a.m. I sigh, a breath laden with affirmation. The right decision was made. My home is here, not a paradox but a sanctuary.

I head to the kitchen to brew a cup of coffee. Hell, I feel like I need more than a few. I open my laptop to see it's still fully charged and go to the chapter I had begun to work on. As I sit with my steamy brew, I decide to scan the news checking as I always did every morning.

Nothing earth-shattering here other than a large earthquake in Turkey and problems at the border crossings. I scroll down to see a short article about a Paul Vlahos, an accomplished scientist who passed away from cancer just two days ago at the age of sixty-three. I go on to read the article, which states that he was recognized for his studies in time travel, astronomy, and astrophysics and had won several accolades for his work. It goes on to say that a special service is being held for him at the Astronomy Department at Penn State next week to honor his work. *I guess he moved on from YSU to finish his grad studies there.*

I shake my head. *He truly was ahead of his time back in the seventies.*

After breakfast, I'm ready to call Brandy to try to explain why I'm not on my way to the airport for my trip. She knows me well, and I'll have to come up with a good one here. She wouldn't be amused if I told her I was whooping it up back in the seventies. She'd most likely hop on a plane to make sure her mother had not gone mad.

I wait after I tell her I'm still at home.

"What's happened, Mom? Why—"

"I'm not ready to do the beach scene without Laney, so I've decided to spend a few days at State College, over by Penn State," I say without hesitation, glancing at my packed suitcases sitting on the bedroom floor, ready for a beach vacation.

"Why? What's there? This just isn't like you!"

"You know that's originally where I wanted to go to school, but with my state of finances, I had to live at home so I could easily commute to YSU. There are some great art galleries and quirky shops there, besides. It's a small town, just the kind of getaway I need," I lie. Some truth finally emerges when I tell her I'll be making a stopover in Ohio to visit my dear friend, Tracey Blaznick, whom I've been promising to visit for years now. A drive up to Mill Creek Park is on the agenda, as well.

I have to make plans to rent a car and drive up there. There's a strong pull inside me to see Lanterman's Mill one more time that I can't deny.

"Well, just as long as it suits you. I do agree that you need to get away, and I'm glad you are getting together with your old friend again. From all the stories you've told about how the two of you used to be band groupies, it'll be good to relive those memories."

I sigh. *If she only knew.*

"I'd love to chat longer, Mom, but I've gotta run to work. Promise you'll call tonight and let me know all the details?"

I think about all of the lies I've told here and back in '76. *Lord, help me! I reason lying might be my newly acquired vice.*

Now, to call Laney and break the news to her. She'll be a bit harder to convince that this trip to PA is just a simple getaway. She's always had this intuition thing about her. I guess that's why we got along so well.

My call goes to her voicemail, and I breathe a sigh of relief. It just gives me more time to come up with a few good excuses.

The phone rings as I head to the bedroom to get dressed. *Who can that be?* With everything that's recently gone on I start to shake.

It's Mark. My heart is in my throat when I hear his strong voice. "Hey, Jenn. I'm glad I caught you."

I remain silent. The shakiness starts to abate.

"You still there?"

"Y…yes, I'm here. What's up?"

"Wanted to see if you'd like to have dinner with me over at Pelican Pointe in Clearwater this weekend. I think we need to talk."

*Did he just ask me out? It's been so long.*

*Does he know about the time travel? Could he have possibly—*

*No.*

*I have to control my thoughts and answer the man.* "Yes, I'd love that, too, Mark, and I agree: we need to talk. I'll be away for a bit but will let you know when I get home."

He responds quickly out of concern, "Is everything okay, Jenn?"

"Yes, all is fine. I'm taking some time off to finish this book and getting away will help." *Ah, another good one.* I smile inwardly.

Our call comes to an end and my mind drifts back to the moment Mark and I first met. The memory surfaces vividly, him at Kent State, his long, green army coat as he steps into the club on that fateful night, and a soft smile graces my lips. There was an immediate attraction that night, chemistry at work, for sure.

When I turn my attention to the neatly packed suitcases awaiting my journey to Virginia Beach, a surge of excitement rushes through me. I reach into the larger one, and my fingers brush against the fabric of an off-the-shoulder black cocktail dress. It's the one I'll wear to meet Mark for dinner when I get back. A sense of anticipation fills the air, the prospect of rekindling something special with him after our separation.

I step into my closet to peruse the modest selection of conservative dresses hanging at the far back. Two catch my eye. Their simplicity and elegance are quite fitting for the service honoring Paul. I take them down with a thoughtful sweep of my hand and lay them on the bed, my mind tracing back to the immense favor Paul did for me. Emotions swell within me. Tears form as I reflect on the enormity of his sacrifice. The memory of him killing Troy to protect me resurfaces, and with it, a question lingers: *did he act out of self-interest, driven by the pursuit of scientific acclaim?*

What matters most now is my attendance at Paul's service. My mind swirls with the thought of making an unprecedented speech, but I know I'd never do such a thing. Most will never know our story, and it will remain that way.

My mind shifts to the upcoming dinner with Mark upon my return and reminisce about the night we first met. I stifle a chuckle, thinking about how I'll most likely shock him when recalling all the vivid details of that night as if it happened only yesterday.

# The Author

https://authorlorrainecarey.blogspot.com/

Lorraine Carey is not only a paranormal enthusiast but has had many unexplained events in her lifetime and has used these as a focal point in her fiction novels.

Most of Carey's books were written during the course of nine years while living in the Caymans with her husband. The island was the perfect inspiration for her.

As a veteran Reading Specialist, Lorraine began to write for Young Adults hoping to inspire young readers. Her students always loved hearing her spooky tales. *Jonathan's Locket* was a finalist in the Wind Dancer Film Contest back in 2014.

Lorraine currently resides in St. Petersburg, Florida where she is a private tutor for young children. She continues to write and is planning on joining up with a paranormal investigative team. Her empathic abilities seem to attract the spirits giving her even more motivation to continue writing.

# Contents


The Inspiration ............................................................3

Chapter 1 ................................................................5

    Dylan Anderson 2023................................................5

Chapter 2 ...............................................................10

    Jennifer 2023 ......................................................10

Chapter 3 ...............................................................13

    Jennifer 2023 ......................................................13

Chapter 4 ...............................................................17

    Dylan 2023 .........................................................17

Chapter 5 ...............................................................19

    Jennifer 2023 ......................................................19

Chapter 6 ...............................................................22

    Jennifer 2023 ......................................................22

Chapter 7 ...............................................................26

    Dylan 2023 .........................................................26

Chapter 8 ...............................................................30

    Jennifer 2023 ......................................................30

Chapter 9 ...............................................................34

    Dylan 2023 .........................................................34

Chapter 10 ..............................................................37

    Dylan 2023 .........................................................37

Chapter 11 ..............................................................41

    Jennifer 2023-1976................................................41

Chapter 12 ..............................................................45

Jennifer ..................................................................45

Chapter 13 ...........................................................49

Dylan 1976 ........................................................49

Chapter 14 ...........................................................52

Jennifer ............................................................52

Chapter 15 ...........................................................56

Chapter 16 ...........................................................61

Chapter 17 ...........................................................65

Chapter 18 ...........................................................71

Chapter 19 ...........................................................76

Chapter 20 ...........................................................82

Chapter 21 ...........................................................85

Chapter 22 ...........................................................89

Chapter 23 ...........................................................94

Chapter 24 ...........................................................98

Chapter 25 .........................................................105

Chapter 26 .........................................................110

Dylan .............................................................110

Chapter 27 .........................................................112

Chapter 28 .........................................................117

Chapter 29 .........................................................123

Chapter 30 .........................................................128

Chapter 31 .........................................................133

Chapter 32 .........................................................141

Chapter 33 .........................................................148

Chapter 34 ..................................................................152

Chapter 35 ..................................................................159

Chapter 36 ..................................................................164

Chapter 37 ..................................................................167

   Jennifer 2023 ..........................................................167

The Author ..................................................................173